FOR WHOM THE BELL TOLLS

Quicker than eyesight, Fargo filled his hand with blue steel. Then, up in the bell tower, he spotted the familiar glint of sunlight on skin. The Colt leaped three times in his hand. His last shot made the bell ring.

At first, when all fell silent, Fargo figured the would-be murderer had fled. Abruptly, a straw-haired man with a chiseled face and shoulders broad as a yoke appeared in the opening of the tower for a moment. Fargo thumb-cocked his Colt, ready to put sunlight through him. Before he could fire, the man suddenly plummeted to the plaza like a sack of dirt, impaling himself on the iron spikes of the church fence. . . .

THE
TRAILSMAN
#330

TUCSON
TEMPTRESS

by
Jon Sharpe

A SIGNET BOOK

SIGNET
Published by New American Library, a division of
Penguin Group (USA) Inc., 375 Hudson Street,
New York, New York 10014, USA
Penguin Group (Canada), 90 Eglinton Avenue East, Suite 700, Toronto,
Ontario M4P 2Y3, Canada (a division of Pearson Penguin Canada Inc.)
Penguin Books Ltd., 80 Strand, London WC2R 0RL, England
Penguin Ireland, 25 St. Stephen's Green, Dublin 2,
Ireland (a division of Penguin Books Ltd.)
Penguin Group (Australia), 250 Camberwell Road, Camberwell, Victoria 3124,
Australia (a division of Pearson Australia Group Pty. Ltd.)
Penguin Books India Pvt. Ltd., 11 Community Centre, Panchsheel Park,
New Delhi - 110 017, India
Penguin Group (NZ), 67 Apollo Drive, Rosedale, North Shore 0632,
New Zealand (a division of Pearson New Zealand Ltd.)
Penguin Books (South Africa) (Pty.) Ltd., 24 Sturdee Avenue,
Rosebank, Johannesburg 2196, South Africa

Penguin Books Ltd., Registered Offices:
80 Strand, London WC2R 0RL, England

First published by Signet, an imprint of New American Library,
a division of Penguin Group (USA) Inc.

First Printing, April 2009
10 9 8 7 6 5 4 3 2 1

The first chapter of this book previously appeared in *Bayou Trackdown*, the three hundred
twenty-ninth volume in this series.

Copyright © Penguin Group (USA) Inc., 2009
All rights reserved

 REGISTERED TRADEMARK—MARCA REGISTRADA

PUBLISHER'S NOTE
This is a work of fiction. Names, characters, places, and incidents either are the product of
the author's imagination or are used fictitiously, and any resemblance to actual persons,
living or dead, business establishments, events, or locales is entirely coincidental.
    The publisher does not have any control over and does not assume any responsibility for
author or third-party Web sites or their content.

The Trailsman

Beginnings . . . they bend the tree and they mark the man. Skye Fargo was born when he was eighteen. Terror was his midwife, vengeance his first cry. Killing spawned Skye Fargo, ruthless, cold-blooded murder. Out of the acrid smoke of gunpowder still hanging in the air, he rose, cried out a promise never forgotten.

The Trailsman they began to call him all across the West: searcher, scout, hunter, the man who could see where others only looked, his skills for hire but not his soul, the man who lived each day to the fullest, yet trailed each tomorrow. Skye Fargo, the Trailsman, the seeker who could take the wildness of a land and the wanting of a woman and make them his own.

Tucson, Arizona Territory, 1860—
where "stranglers" rule supreme and a beautiful woman's
embrace is the dance of death.

1

The sound of gunfire ripped through the furnace-hot desert air, but the lone, crop-bearded rider astride a black-and-white pinto stallion ignored it. One or two shots, the rider mused idly, usually meant celebration fire, just drunks hurrahing the town. Three or more often meant somebody was six feet closer to hell.

"Time to tank up, old campaigner," Skye Fargo told the stallion, reining in at a small spring just outside the siesta-prone, but dangerous, settlement of Tucson in south-central Arizona Territory.

Fargo had been feeling a case of the nervous fantods for the past twenty miles or so. With the bluecoat pony soldiers being pulled from nearby Camp Grant for the rumored war brewing back east, three dangerous tribes—Comanche, Kiowa, and Apache—were making life hell for everyone else out here.

Fargo dipped his dusty head into the cool spring water, then cupped handfuls and drank them. Next he dropped the Ovaro's bridle and let him drink. More gunfire erupted from town, and Fargo thumbed back the rawhide riding thong from the hammer of his single-action Colt.

"Don't go looking for your own grave," he muttered, advice from a Ute warrior, up in the Mormon country, just before the Ute almost killed him. But when had the Trailsman, as some called Fargo, ever done the *safe* thing?

Fargo studied Tucson and the surrounding terrain from slitted eyes, a tall, rangy, sinew-tough man wearing buckskins and a wide-brimmed plainsman's hat. His face was tanned hickory-nut brown above the darker brown of his beard. Eyes the pure blue of a mountain lake stayed in constant motion.

Fargo didn't like what he was seeing—and not seeing. In places sagebrush grew tall enough to hide a man, and as Fargo had ridden across the dreaded desert of southern Arizona Territory in the past

1

few days, he had spotted rock mounds where victims of Indian attack had been buried—killed by Apaches, most likely.

But the view within the town limits was just as ominous. At first glance, all Fargo could see through blurry heat waves was the steeple of massive San Antonio church at the head of the central plaza. A green expanse of barley land ringed the town, cultivation meeting the desert like a knife edge. Strips of cottonwood lined the little Santa Cruz River, which divided the narrow and fertile valley where the mining-supply center of Tucson was located.

None of that, however, impressed Fargo as much as the slumping body hanging from a cottonwood limb near the river. He couldn't read the sign pinned to it, so he retrieved his brass binoculars from a saddle pocket.

"Jerked to Jesus," he read aloud, shaking his head in disgust.

There were no Rangers out here as had recently been formed in Texas, and not enough marshals to fill an outhouse. Fargo had been warned, before he left Fort Yuma, about Tucson's notorious Committee for Public Safety. Furthermore, he vastly preferred the Arizona Territory as it looked farther north, a mostly unpopulated landscape of pine trees, granite cliffs, and air that didn't cling in your lungs like molten glass.

But Fargo was a victim of events. He had recently lost a high-stakes match against a pretty redhead who ran a faro wheel, and a sorely needed job as a fast-messenger rider awaited him here.

Fargo snugged the bridle again, the Ovaro taking the bit easily, and swung up into leather. He took a moment to slide his 16-shot Henry rifle from its saddle scabbard and check the vulnerable tube magazine for dents. Then he spurred the Ovaro forward, aiming for the central plaza at the heart of town.

Not much had changed, Fargo quickly realized, since last time he'd ridden these unpaved, sun-drenched streets. Lumber was scarce in the region, and most of the buildings were of Indian-style puddled adobe with brush ramadas shading the doors. Not one hotel or store, but plenty of twenty-four-hour gambling houses. Fargo heard lilting Spanish everywhere. The place was still overrun with dogs, whose constant yapping made the Ovaro stutter-step nervously.

When Fargo's eyes flicked to the rammed-earth sidewalks, the two-legged curs watching him from hooded glances bothered him even more. The local vigilantes were as obvious as bedbugs on a clean sheet, for they all carried double-ten scatterguns, barrels sawed off to ten inches.

"Mr. Fargo? Mr. Skye Fargo?"

At the sound of a musical female voice, Fargo tugged rein and slued around in the saddle. A young woman stood in the doorway of a two-story adobe house that fronted on the plaza. The room visible behind her seemed almost bare, but clean, darned curtains hung in the windows. Seeing him rein in, she began running toward him—and she "jiggled" impressively, Fargo noticed.

"Mr. Fargo?" she asked again.

Fargo opened his mouth to reply, but as he got a better look at her he was struck dumb by this sensuous vision. The Trailsman was no novice when it came to rating woman flesh, and he figured this one was at the top of the heap—far as her looks, anyway. Horn combs held her long, russet hair neatly in place, and her figure showed to curving perfection in a pinch-waist gown of emerald green silk and lace.

"Mr. Skye Fargo?" she repeated, stopping beside the Ovaro and shading her eyes with one hand to look up at him.

In the seductive style of Santa Fe women, kohl had been artfully applied to lengthen her eyebrows, shade the lids, and extend the outer corners of the eyes. Fargo felt sudden loin warmth and was forced to discreetly shift in the saddle. He was rarely woman starved, but he often got plenty hungry.

"Excuse my bad parlor manners, miss," Fargo hastened to say, tipping his hat. "Yes, I'm Skye Fargo. May I ask how you know me?"

"Mr. Fargo, you're too modest. Any western school child can tell you about the fearless Trailsman."

Fargo grinned, strong white teeth flashing through his beard. "School child? Well, if that includes you, maybe I'll get an education, Miss . . . ?"

"Oh, forgive me. I'm Amy Hanchon. My father, he . . ."

She faltered and Fargo waited patiently. The bell of San Antonio sounded the hour, three p.m. Wagon teams constantly brought in loads of merchant stock, and now there were a dozen or so wagons parked in the plaza as the teamsters slept. Fargo spotted at least one vigilante in the shadow of the east plaza, watching him from eyes fatal as a snake.

"My father," she soldiered on bravely, knuckling away a sudden

3

tear, "is Daniel Hanchon. Reverend Daniel Hanchon. He is . . . was also a silver miner with political aspirations. But now I'm getting ahead of myself. Mr. Fargo, would you consider working for me?"

Fargo reluctantly pried his eyes away from the creamy white swells of her bosoms, thrust high by tight stays.

"First of all, Amy, I'm curious. Even if you have heard some backcountry lore about me, how could you recognize me riding past your house? I don't pose for portraits."

"Because of the *Tucson Intelligencer*, our newspaper. You see, I tried to place a notice for the services of hired guns. The editor was sympathetic, but he was afraid to do it."

Her pretty face tightened with bitterness. "He's afraid of Henry Lutz and that despicable goon of his, Crawley Lake. Every 'man' in this region spits when Lutz says hawk."

Fargo slanted a glance toward the vigilante in the shadows. He was looking north toward the huge church. Fargo felt a warning tingle in his scalp. Very soon he would regret not heeding it.

"Henry Lutz," he repeated. "Would that be Bearcat Lutz?"

"Yes! You know him?"

Fargo shook his head. "Know of him, is all. I hear he's the self-appointed head of the Tucson Committee for Public Safety. Anyhow, you were saying the newspaper editor was scared?"

"Yes, because I'm daring to defy Lutz. But the editor heard you were headed to Tucson to take a job with the Butterfield Overland. He said every newspaperman west of the Mississippi has heard of you."

"Yeah, I've been blessed all to hell," Fargo said from a deadpan. "But you're taking the long way around the barn, Amy. What's your dicker with Lutz?"

"He's my father's chief business rival. They are also bitter political rivals, each with a faction supporting them for Territorial Governor. Lutz is a cold-blooded murderer, but my father is the local Methodist minister, and even Lutz is afraid to openly murder a man of God. So he used his 'authority' as head of the vigilantes and arrested my father on a trumped-up charge of rape. He even paid a young Mexican girl, his own whore—I mean, mistress—to testify at the so-called miners' court."

"You're sure there's no truth to the charge?"

Red spots of anger leaped into her cheeks. "It's pure buncombe!"

4

"It's rough business, falling into the hands of stranglers," Fargo allowed, using the common Southwest word for vigilantes. "But you need law, not me."

She placed her hands lightly on her hips. "What law? I doubt you know the half about Henry Lutz. Don't think my father is sitting in jail, Mr. Fargo. Lutz and his lick-spittles are arresting almost any man who drifts into Tucson, accusing them of peddling whiskey to the Apaches."

"That's an easy pitch right now," Fargo said. "Apaches have wiped out every white settlement except this one."

"Exactly. The prisoners spend their nights in Lutz's private prison, but from dawn until late night they work in his silver mine."

She pointed to a blue-gray line of foothills about two miles north of town. "The prison is conveniently close to the mine. So long as a man can do the donkey work, he stays alive. When he finally breaks, he's sentenced and executed. Locals are starting to call Tucson 'Hangtown.' My father is a strong man, but he's no longer young."

"I take it you want me to break him out?"

"Oh, *yes*! If he can be taken east where there's law, Lutz can't touch him. Will you do it, Mr. Fargo? Please . . . Skye?"

Fargo cursed silently. He'd rather buy ready-to-wear boots than lock horns with a criminal army. Besides, there was a contract with his name on it waiting at the Butterfield Overland office, a job that would mostly keep him away from the rattle and hullabaloo of cities.

"Lady," he finally said, "looks to me like Bearcat has the whip-hand while you're trying to kick the dirt out from under your own feet. There's still soldiers at Camp Grant."

"Yes, but many are being called back east. And my father swears the commander is on Lutz's payroll."

"Even so, the plan you're backing just gives stranglers all the ammo they need to make more arrests. These hemp-committee types are gutter filth, and they *will* hang a woman—after they've had their use of her."

"That will surely happen," she warned, "if you just ride away like it's none of your business. You're the Trailsman, a supposedly brave man who takes on lost causes and wins. They say you can sniff out a rat in a pile of garbage."

"Well, 'they' make me out all wrong. I'm not the law, and I

5

don't go sniffing for rats—I prefer to avoid them. This Lutz sounds like a hard twist, all right, but you'll need a badge-toter to help you. Right now I plan to exercise my liver."

Fargo tipped his hat and took up the slack in the reins. But before he could thump the Ovaro forward, Amy laughed bitterly.

"Oh, I see. Another sawdust Casanova," she dismissed him. "It's all lies about your courage. Devilment is all you men seek."

Fargo grinned wide. "And I s'pose you're purer than Caesar's wife?"

"You've probably had her, too." Amy stamped her foot in anger. "Perverse, arrogant, and uncouth," she summed him up. A moment later, watching him, she added, "If your stupid grin grows any wider, you'll rip your cheeks."

"Tell you the straight, that acid tongue doesn't help your disposition any," Fargo retorted. "Why don't we—"

Just then the Ovaro nickered, side-stepping nervously. Fargo swallowed his sentence without finishing it, remembering the vigilante across the plaza. Fargo spotted him just as a rifle somewhere above the plaza spoke its piece, the sound whip-cracking through the lazy air.

He felt the wind-rip when a lethally close bullet snapped past his face and chewed into the baked mud of the plaza, only inches from a shocked Amy. Fargo saw her leap like a butt-shot dog, then foolishly freeze in place instead of seeking cover.

The shooter opened up in earnest, a hammering racket of gunfire. Fargo hated to do it, but rounds were peppering them nineteen-to-the-dozen, and his experienced eye told him it was Amy the shooter was after, not him—yet, fear froze her in place like a pillar of salt. So Fargo, hunched low in the saddle, planted his left boot on her chest and gave a mighty shove.

The thrust catapulted her backward and out of immediate danger, but now the hidden shooter opened up with a vengeance on Fargo. A round whacked into his saddle, another tugged his hat off. By now, however, Fargo had followed the bullets back to their source—the bell tower of San Antonio church.

It was a job best suited for the Henry, but fractional seconds counted now, and Fargo knew his belt gun would be faster. Quicker than eyesight, he filled his hand with blue steel. Just then, up in the bell tower, he spotted the familiar glint of sunlight on skin. The Colt leaped three times in his hand. His last shot made the bell ring.

At first, when all fell silent, Fargo figured the would-be murderer had fled. Abruptly, a straw-haired man with a chiseled face and shoulders broad as a yoke appeared in the opening of the tower for a moment. Fargo thumb-cocked his Colt, ready to put sunlight through him. Before he could fire, the man suddenly plummeted to the plaza like a sack of dirt, impaling himself on the iron spikes of the church fence.

"Gone to hunt the white buffalo," Fargo muttered, leathering his six-gun. A second later a woman's shrill, piercing scream startled the yapping dogs silent.

2

Fargo helped a shaken Amy up from the adobe brick. Only moments after Fargo's last shot, a man in a tall plug hat emerged from a prosperous-looking undertaker's parlor with a big canvas awning out front. He scurried across the plaza toward the church, perhaps to beat competitors to the body.

"You all right?" Fargo asked the girl, picking up his hat.

"Yes, thanks to you. Look! A bullet pierced my gown."

Amy, who could not see all that happened after Fargo pushed her down, craned her neck toward the church. "Is he . . . ?"

"Cold as a basement floor," Fargo confirmed.

He cast a quick glance around the plaza. Two vigilantes with their sawed-off scatterguns hurried toward the body.

Fargo grabbed the Ovaro's reins. "We best skedaddle back to your place. I'm damned if I'll let these cheapjack 'deputies' arrest me."

Amy paled. "My house? Skye, you need to leave town *now*. That's likely a Committee man you killed."

Fargo shook his head as he began leading the Ovaro away. "Leaving town is all right for me, sure. My stallion gallops like his Pa's name is Going and his Ma's name is Fast. None of these bucket bellies in town could take the pace or follow my trail. But, with stranglers, it's best to take the bull by the horns. Amy, it's not me that man tried to kill just now. He was after you."

Her heart-shaped lips parted in surprise. "Me? Are you sure?"

Fargo nodded, stepping up the pace before the vigilantes drank some Dutch courage and swarmed on him. "Shot patterns prove it. I didn't get fired at until I pushed you out of the way and made the shooter mad."

Amy's brilliant blue eyes misted. "You saved my life back there after all the horrid things I said about you."

"Horrid? Lady, you just scratched the surface. Besides, I'd reckon that a woman trying to save her father has plenty to fret about."

"But, why kill me? They already have father, and a woman is powerless this far west."

"They must've seen us together and twigged the game. They went after you figuring I'd ride on once my employer was killed. Kill me instead, and they'll have to kill the next gun you hire—maybe even a Pinkerton man."

Amy nodded, her pretty face serious. "Yes, that's sensible. And woman or not, I'm Father's confidante in all matters. I know too much about Henry Lutz's nefarious operation."

Fargo cast a cross-shoulder glance toward San Antonio church at the head of the big central plaza. Every saloon in town, and there were several on each side of the plaza, was doing a land-office business. But in born-on-the-spot towns like Tucson, Fargo knew, men seldom had real fun—they engaged in grim, determined dissipation, and no distraction was more welcome than a killing. Men spilled from all the saloons, flocking to see the skewered body on the fence.

"They're pointing this way," Fargo said. "Don't speed up. Let them see we're not running. Got a livery close by?"

"This way," Amy said, tugging him into a shadowed alley of deep-rutted dirt.

An old Mexican with sun-bronzed skin and very little English ran a cottonwood log livery stable where the alley met deserted Silver Street.

"Trim the feet," Fargo instructed the old hostler in a mix of Spanish and English, flipping him a gold dollar. "Then nail the rear offside shoe on tighter—I can hear it clicking. He'll need a rubdown, too, but don't forget he's uncut—don't stand behind him."

"*Claro, Senor.*"

Fargo stalled the Ovaro, stripped off the tack, then forked hay into the canvas net and filled the wooden water pail from a pump in the yard. During all this, Amy stayed in the alley watching for pursuers.

"That's a good sign," Fargo said when they made it back to her house without incident. "They're unsure of me and had to go to their boss."

"That won't take them long," Amy said. She pointed to the opposite side of the plaza and one of the few lumber houses in town. "That's Lutz's house. Notice the turrets and the slate roof. Befitting our next governor-king," she added sarcastically.

Fargo stepped in behind her, dropped his saddle behind the door, then slid the heavy iron bar into its locking braces across the door. As with most dobies in the Spanish style, a Judas hole in the front door allowed a view to the front.

"Any other doors?" Fargo asked.

She shook her head. "You think they'll come here?"

"They have to. If they let me off the hook, they lose their authority."

The bells of San Antonio, unfazed by the earlier gunplay, rang four times. Amy led him from the stone-flagged entranceway into the roomy main salon of the house. The place looked solid enough, but Fargo had seen hard rain turn adobe into puddles of mud and straw. As in most houses in the remote Southwest, the furnishings were sparse. A hidebound trunk, serving as a small table, an embroidered fire screen, and several rawhide-patched chairs made up most of the room's furnishings.

"I'm sorry the place looks so empty," she told him. "It's not easy to haul in furniture, what with deserts and warpath Indians."

"I never owned a stick of furniture in my life," Fargo admitted. "So you're doing fine."

"At least the beds are of good quality," she added, sending him a veiled glance, and Fargo felt his lips twitch into a grin.

"A man can't praise a good bed too much," he agreed.

"I was talking about sleeping, of course."

"I wasn't," Fargo admitted. "You offended?"

She replied with a mysterious smile. Fargo propped his Henry against the nearest wall and retrieved the extra cylinder of ammunition from a saddle pocket, laying it beside the rifle.

"This Lutz character," he coaxed her, "how far will he go to get what he wants?"

"As far as he needs to. He requires only a tissue-paper pretext to arrest someone. He's no halfway man, that's certain. Back in Illinois, we called men like him katydid boosters—wildly optimistic about opportunities out West. But Lutz goes much farther."

"Yeah, I've met the type more than I care to," Fargo said. "Out here in sagebrush country they're called howlers."

"By any name, Judge Moneybags runs this town."

Fargo only nodded, having seen human cesspools too often in his travels throughout the West. In towns like Tucson, Laredo, and Los Angeles, owlhoots on the dodge were safe to maraud while the honest citizens cowered in their homes.

Fargo moved to a front window and peeled back a corner of the curtain to gaze outside. "What about Lutz's toadies?" he asked.

"My father's convinced that most of them are stupid stumblebums. But Crawley Lake, his . . . foreman, I guess you'd call him, is very dangerous. A despicable killer. He once raped a Mexican nun, then hanged her for fornication, just to scare the church into silence. It worked."

Fargo glanced back and watched her pacing nervously, hips swaying in rhythmic motion. He felt a warm flush of desire and reluctantly looked away again. This was no time for the giddy dance.

"Lutz has been swaggering it around since he arrived, acting ten inches taller than God," Amy resumed. "Dad saw the town going to hell on a fast horse. He started writing letters to Washington City and to newspapers in Santa Fe, Salt Lake City, and St. Louis. I guess he finally pushed Lutz too far."

Fargo spotted a group of five men angling across the plaza toward the Hanchon residence. Four of them carried the familiar express guns.

"Looks like company coming," he warned Amy. "Stay calm and don't be fooled by anything unpleasant I might say or do. I can't kill all these men at once, plus we need to buy some time, so this will need wit and wile."

A demanding fist rocked the door on its leather hinges. "Fargo!" bellowed a deep voice like gravel shifting in a rusty hold. "Fargo, you're even stupider than God made you! You just murdered a regulator! Open this door!"

"That's Crawley Lake," Amy whispered to Fargo.

"The names change," Fargo replied, "but never the cockroaches."

He could see the speaker through the Judas hole, a towering slab of muscle with a flat face like a sandstone carving, curiously pale and incomplete. Several human ears were pinned to his shirt. The dapper man beside him, wearing a rawhide vest and octagonal tie with a clean white shirt, had to be Lutz. Most men Fargo met had one of those faces forgotten the moment he saw it. Not Henry

"Bearcat" Lutz. The features were shrewd, heartless, grasping, and tinged with murderous excess.

Again Lake pounded on the door. "Sorry to spoil your big time, stud horse. Time to button your fly and get yourself boosted branchward. Now open up!"

"Oh, I intend to open up," Fargo called back. "Makes it easier to kill you. But there'll be some rules first."

"*Rules?* Fargo, are you soft between your head handles? You ain't the big he-bear here."

"Pipe down, Crawley," Lutz interceded. "Let's hear your rules, Mr. Fargo."

"Just two. All those double-tens will be left outside. You can keep your short-irons, but I'll make a sieve out of the first bastard who clears leather."

Crawley started to bluster, but Lutz spoke over him. "Agreed, Fargo. If any man draws on you, you can kill him for cause."

Fargo waited until all four scatterguns had been grounded. He lifted the bar aside, shucked out his Colt, and threw the door wide.

"C'mon in, boys," he called out affably.

"This won't be a sitting-down visit," Amy added, eyeing Lutz with cool distaste. "Just state your business."

"The cow's bellowin' to the bulls," Crawley said as the five men edged carefully inside. Crawley's reptilian eyes slithered all over Amy.

"Is she your fancy piece, Fargo?" he demanded. "I always meant to point her heels to the sky, but I'm damned if I'll take *your* leavings."

Amy slanted a quelling stare toward Crawley. But the angry bear of a man was staring at Fargo. "Big man in buckskins, anh? A regular gunologist, I hear. Good thing for you that barking iron ain't in your holster."

"You mean, like this?"

Fargo spun the weapon back into the holster. "Always happy to oblige. The rest of you gents stand aside. Amy, you, too. Let's open the ball, Crawley."

Crawley's right hand twitched as he rested it on the walnut butt of his Volcanic pistol. "Don't come swingin' your eggs around here, mister. They'll get snipped off."

"That's right, stranger," one of the other three vigilantes piped up. "You might say Crawley here is a depopulation expert."

"So your boss is double rough, is that it? Then go ahead and slap leather," Fargo invited again, his gaze as steady as his breathing and speech.

Crawley's gun hand continued to twitch while he stood silent.

"Those ears pinned to your shirt don't scare a papoose. *Jerk* that smoke wagon," Fargo said, his eyes hard and piercing.

"All in good time, puke pail. I could paper these walls with your brains if I wanted." Eyes smoky with rage, Crawley turned away.

"Oh, I get it," Fargo said. "You *talk* like the big stallion, but you always get a sore hoof when it's time to saddle up."

"Never mind this clash of stags," Lutz cut in. "Mr. Fargo, you murdered one of my men."

Fargo laughed. "You see any green on my antlers? That murder charge is horse shit, and you know it. The law is clear in the Territories: There is no duty to retreat if attacked. Miss Hanchon and I were fired on first."

"So you *say*. Witnesses claim you were clearly ordered to throw down your weapons."

"That never happened. But even if it had, no ragtag vigilantes have authority to disarm a man. Only U.S. marshals and the army can do that."

Lutz chuckled, right thumb and forefinger stroking his goatee. "Can't wait on them. Fargo, you're a relic. Your kind died out when the last beaver streams out here were trapped out by the 1830s. Hell, I've heard about you. You're a wild mustang roaming the West—a bunch-quitter. Towns, to you, mean women, whiskey, a hot steak. But I intend to roost here, and that means law and order."

Fargo had noticed Amy struggling to follow his order about remaining silent. Now, however, her anger and frustration erupted.

"Law and order?" she repeated. "Lutz, your plans are general knowledge. You require non-Indian labor for your mine, and you hate paying for it. So you've 'arrested' my father, one of the best men in this pitiless town, and dozens more and condemned them to hard labor. You also plan, in violation of federal law, to exterminate or at least permanently drive off the Apache Eskiminzin and his band."

Lutz winked at Fargo. "Brash as a government mule, isn't she? I *like* a woman with starch in her corset."

"Me, too," Crawley chimed in. "The feisty ones crawl all over you in bed."

Lutz turned to Amy. "Your father *was* also a good miner, sugar corset. But he's a buttinsky, a crusader."

"Don't forget rapist," Fargo reminded him from a poker face.

"That, too, of course."

"Filthy, sordid lies!" Amy cried out. "You paid your own mistress to say Father raped her."

Lutz smiled with smug patience. "Amy, like your father, you're too headstrong to get the point. Said an ancient Egytian pharaoh, 'Happy is the man who does what he is told.'"

"That includes you?" Fargo asked.

Bearcat shook his head. "I'm a rainmaker, Fargo. Now, it's true you did a good job of gelding Crawley just now. But, no offense, I can draw for thousands while broken-heeled saddle tramps like you can't afford a busted trace chain."

One of the three thugs sized up Fargo, his right hand moving to touch his holster.

"Go ahead," Fargo invited in his cordial tone. "One of you clear leather. Oh, I'll eventually die of lead poisoning, but so will at least three of you—starting with the Bearcat here."

"Stevens!" Lutz snapped. "You're walking on your own grave—and mine. Forget it."

Fargo resumed as if nothing had intervened. "It's true I don't have two nickels to rub together. But I can be mighty useful to a man that does."

Startled, Lutz's shrewd eyes swept over the tall man in faded buckskins. Before he could reply, however, an agitated Amy turned her fiery-eyed wrath on Lutz.

"Mr. Lutz, how can you imprison my father without bail and a trial?"

Now Lutz's eyes were bland and innocent. "Murder and rape are both non-bailable offenses in the Territories. Ask your friend Fargo, *he* seems to be an expert on the law. As for a trial—your old man will get one when the circuit judge rides in. Given the Apache menace, that will be months from now."

"*If* he makes it," Crawley tossed in. "This is a dangerous place."

Amy couldn't restrain her anger. "Lutz, who are you to seize authority as if you have some right to do so? Your 'committee' has no legal authority, nor does your prison. You're running a slave-labor camp."

Lutz waved this aside. "You seem to have more conclusions than facts to warrant them. Look around, missy. White people in Tucson have money to toss at the birds. Even the Mexers have jobs thanks to men like me. Take your sweetheart's new job with Butterfield—mail delivered twice weekly since 1857. That's some pumpkins. When I first staked my claim, all we had was jackass mail whenever it got through. That's *progress*, Miss Hanchon, the kind the American West needs. You'd best take the temperature of the water before you rock the boat."

For strategic reasons Fargo said nothing, but he knew all about the howlers and their "progress." He had watched their hydraulic mining wash away mountains, their lumber crews strip so many slopes bare that towns below were washed away in mud slides. Fargo was all for making a dollar, but not at the price of the pristine American West—all of which he considered his home.

Lutz, however, was evidently still mulling the Trailsman's last, surprising remark.

"Fargo," he said, "I like to come right out of the chute bucking. One of my men has gone up the flume thanks to you. How'd you like to work for me and make up the loss?"

"Boss, are you grazing peyote?" Crawley demanded.

"Not at all. Fargo knows more about local Indians than any white man alive, and his trailcraft is said to be unmatched. You, Crawley, have done nothing to solve our little problem with the Apaches. Maybe he can."

"It's tempting," Fargo admitted, and Amy's mouth fell open. "Give me a night to think on it. After all, I gave my word to the Butterfield folks."

"Huh," Crawley said to his boss. "That shitheel ain't got the caliber for the job. And how we gonna trust him? Hell, he just sent one of our men to the farther side of Jordan. Might be a damn spy."

"Oh, it's risky," Lutz agreed. "But you have to bet big to win big. Besides, the man who can back you down, Crawley, is worth putting on the payroll. But, Fargo, a word to the wise is sufficient: For a rebel there is no tomb, nor even a nameless grave."

"Or to put it less like a book talking," Crawley clarified, "any man who defies Bearcat Lutz—or *me*—buys the farm, bull and all. How you like *them* apples, buckskin boy?"

"That's gaudy patter," Fargo said. "Real flashy."

"Call on me tomorrow morning at my place," Lutz told Fargo as the five visitors trooped outside into the mellow sunlight of late afternoon.

Crawley Lake, his flat, sandstone face brooding, turned in the doorway to stare at Fargo. "You rolled a seven today, cockchafer. But luck don't last long in Tucson. Make one fox play against us, and you'll be the sorriest son of a bitch on the continent. Matter fact, you best pull foot now, or your fancy piece will be picking lead out of your sitter."

3

"Has your brain come unhinged?" Amy demanded as Fargo kept an eye on the retreating men.

"Always surprise, mystify, and confuse your enemies," he replied.

"Well, you're doing a good job of all that on *me*, too."

Fargo grinned, letting the curtain fall back. "You haven't proved yet you're not my enemy."

For a moment her worried face transformed itself into a come-hither smile. "That's your job. I've always believed men are granted no desires that can't be satisfied. Women, too."

Fargo took that as an invitation on a silver platter, but hard-won survival instinct kept him at the window a little longer.

"Asking Lutz for work was reckless," Fargo conceded. "But face it—right now we're neither up the well nor down. We've *got* to make a move, and this might give me access to your father."

"Surely to God you can't be serious? You'll be shot in the back."

"There's that, yeah. But look at the odds. With the numbers stacked so high against us, rearguard actions won't get it done."

"Sounds like you know your business," she relented, wringing her hands nervously.

Fargo finally leathered his six-shooter and left the window, slacking into one of the rawhide-patched chairs and scrubbing his face with his hands. He felt stiff and saddle sore. He'd been on a hot, dangerous trail since dawn, and felt his stomach pinch with hunger.

"My manners!" Amy exclaimed, bustling toward the rear of the house. "I'll fix us a bite. There's some *pulque* in that wall cabinet. Dad loves it, but I think it tastes bitter."

Fargo would have preferred a few jolts of wagon-yard whiskey, but cactus liquor did the job, too, and right now he needed a bracer. True, he'd jumped over a snake just now. But Bearcat Lutz and Crawley Lake were two of the hardest twists he'd ever seen, and the sledding was going to get a lot harder.

Fargo took a decanter of milky liquid from the cabinet and returned to the chair, letting a long pull from the decanter burn a path to his empty belly.

"I apologize for the humble fare," Amy said when she returned carrying a serving tray. "Father and I keep a Spartan larder thanks to the Apache raids on freighters."

She set down steaming bowls of black beans and a plate of blue-corn tortillas.

"If you're hungry enough," Fargo assured her, "a mule becomes a Missouri elk."

He tied into the meal while she only picked at her food.

"Skye? Will they be back?"

"That depends on how much Lutz controls Crawley. Right now Lutz seems interested in hiring me, and I don't see any pressing reason why he needs to kill you—yet. If anybody comes back here, it'll be on Crawley's say-so, not Lutz's."

"Well, I learned today there's no better man to handle him than you. I saw how you backed him down. One of the male passengers in our stagecoach, when Father and I traveled out here, said you were 'absolutely destitute' of physical fear."

"Well, he got the destitute part right." Fargo laughed, swiping at his beans with a piece of tortilla. "Do I walk on water, too? You set out good grub, lady."

"Thank you, but all this hugger-mugger upsets my digestion," Amy complained, pushing her bowl away.

"Sure does," Fargo agreed. "Mind if I eat that?"

"Of course not. You know, Dad calls men like you fiddle-footed—given to wanderlust. We traveled a lot ourselves after mother was killed by consumption. Believe it or not, in France I'm welcome in the chateaux of the nobility."

Fargo stopped chewing and said, "That's fine when you're in France, but it cuts no ice out here in the old Spanish land-grant country. It's root hog or die in these parts and no place for a fine-haired woman."

"Yes, I realize that now. But I'm going nowhere without Father. You *are* going to help me, Skye?"

"I've already started, haven't I? Might's well finish it."

"Oh, Skye, *thank* you, I—"

"Look, don't go tacking up bunting just yet. This is going to be a rough piece of work. There's maybe one U.S. marshal within a ten-days' ride, and the soldiers at Camp Grant are cut to a few companies by transfers back east. Another thing, if I'm giving up a good contract with Butterfield, I'll need pay right off."

Amy's sweetheart lips pressed into a frown. One russet strand of hair had worked loose from the horn comb and curled onto her right cheek in the shape of a comma.

"As to that," she replied, "I admit that, at the moment, I find myself in somewhat straitened circumstances. You see, Father and I have a good silver mine, and—"

"*Had* a good mine," Fargo cut her off. "When stranglers 'arrest' a man, they don't recognize his claim, they take it."

"For the moment, yes. But now you're here. Once you've brought these jackals to justice and freed father, the mine will be ours again and I'll pay you quite generously."

Fargo snorted. "Just that easy, huh? Hell, pink-shell castles for everybody. Lady, this isn't some penny dreadful in *Police Gazette*. These are kill-crazy cutthroats and they surround us. We could both end up cold as a fish on ice, and dead men don't collect wages."

"No," she agreed, breathing deeply to swell her ample bosoms even more, "but living men can enjoy advances on them, right? In the form of . . . barter?"

"Can't it just be for fun? I prefer volunteers."

"For fun then. It's been a long time for me. As for *you*, they say the Trailsman goes through women like a bee sampling flowers."

Fargo folded his arms over his chest. "Don't believe saloon gossip."

She pouted. "It's only gossip? And here I was hoping it might be my turn to be . . . sampled."

By now a copper sunset blazed out on the rim of creation, visible even through the curtains. It flared out in mere moments, and day dozed into night. Amy lit a tallow candle, and their faces seemed to flicker in its uncertain light.

"You lead the way," Fargo told her, standing up. It had been a long time for him, too, and those sensuous hips of hers were priming the pump. Nonetheless, he was clearheaded enough to gather up his brass-framed Henry and the extra ammo cylinder for his Colt.

19

"Will we be safe upstairs?" Amy asked him.

"There's only one door, and it's got a solid bar. The windows are mullioned, so anybody breaking in has to bust glass and the wood frames. We'll hear that. Besides, if Lutz wants my services bad enough, we're prob'ly safe for now."

"I'm sorry to say I dare not ask you to stay here more than one night," Amy told him, leading him up a pine staircase. "Lutz's Committee for Public Safety also oversees 'moral turpitude.' Any unmarried woman 'consorting' with a man is banished from Tucson or forced to license herself as a whore. But there is a lean-to room off the back of the house, perhaps—"

"No thanks. I'll just be digging my own grave if I stay anyplace where the stranglers know I am. Since there's no hotels, I'll be camping outside the town or maybe in the livery corral."

"But the Apaches—"

Fargo silenced her with a hand on the taut curve of her back. "That's the way of it, so never mind Apaches. And don't be such a worrywart."

On the landing, Fargo kissed her, unleashing a feminine torrent of pent-up desire. She leaned into him, moaning, then took his hand and hurried to a nearby bedroom. Despite the severe shortage of good furniture in Tucson, Daniel Hanchon made sure his daughter had a fine rosewood bed with a feather mattress.

"Let's make the first one fast and hard," Amy begged him, setting the candle on a wall shelf. "Never mind clothes."

She pulled the bodice of her gown down, releasing huge, creamy breasts. Then she hiked her gown up and tugged off her frilly pantaloons, opening her legs wide to tease Fargo. He felt his manhood pressing for release as he gazed into her glistening coral grotto. Her bush, a shade darker than the russet hair on her head, was a silky "V" directing his eye to the swollen pearl that proved her arousal.

"I showed you mine," she teased. "Now let's see yours."

He tugged open his fly and released his man gland, making her jaw drop at the sight. "My God, will I be safe with that inside me?"

"I've never had a complaint yet," Fargo assured her, positioning himself in the creamy saddle of her spread-open legs and lining himself up with her nether portal before a thrust of his hips shoved him in to the hilt.

Hot, tickling pleasure seized his entire length as Amy began to mewl and thrash. Fargo obliged her request by stroking her hard and fast, licking and sucking her strawberry nipples stiff.

"Oh, *lord*, Skye!" she gasped, jackknifing up from the bed when several climaxes ripped through her. "It feels like you're in up to my belly button! Oh, *oh*, yes, yes, like that, oh, *do* me deeper!"

Fargo admired erotic appetite in a woman, and her wanton cries were like kerosene on flames. He plunged harder, faster, and she keened even louder, wrapping her legs around him tight and milking his shaft with her love muscle. Fargo felt a familiar warning prickle in his groin and went into the strong finish, exploding inside her and needing a half-dozen more thrusts to spend himself.

Both of them were so exhausted by their intensity that neither moved for at least fifteen minutes.

"Honey," Fargo finally managed just before he tumbled over the threshold into sleep, "you're a mighty potent force."

A rose-tinted sunrise woke Fargo the moment it tinged the bedroom window. He and Amy had played two-backed beast throughout the night, napping and then taking their pleasure yet again, and now he deliberately avoided looking at her naked, smooth-as-lotion skin while he pulled on his boots and buckled on his Colt and shell belt. Now was the time for exerting himself against the enemy.

"Skye," her sleepy voice called to him, "just one more to start the day nice?"

"Lady, if I was ever tempted. But I need to go see Lutz this morning, and before I do that I want to take a squint around. I like to scout an area first before I turn myself into a target."

"Just as well—I *am* a little sore this morning," Amy admitted. "But it's a nice kind of sore."

She sat up, holding the sheet in front of her. "Skye, you be *very* careful. Any man Lutz turns against is arrested as a 'whiskey smuggler' by Crawley Lake. The next step is either hanging or forced labor in the Lady Luck mine."

"I take it Lady Luck is Bearcat's silver mine?"

She nodded, worry clouds marring her face. "Where my father is just now starting work for the day. Lutz will work him to death."

"We'll see about that. B'lieve me, I will be careful. I've locked horns with Lutz's ilk before. Prideful men with no real ability or accomplishments to justify that pride except brazen crimes. That's why they only thrive in the Territories where law is scarce as hen's teeth."

21

Amy pulled on a dressing gown and quickly tugged her hair back into a neat coil. Downstairs, she made coffee while Fargo rummaged in a saddle pocket for a bore brush and ran it through the Colt's muzzle. Then, familiar with the grit-laden wind of Tucson's surrounding deserts, Fargo took out his canvas duster and put it on to protect his Colt and shells.

After a quick breakfast of coffee and mesquite bread, Fargo let himself out carefully onto the plaza and glanced warily around in the cool morning air. The only soul stirring was an old Mexican with a wooden cart filled with pails of water—there were a few wells in Tucson, but most locals bought their water.

Fargo found the liveryman still asleep in one of the stalls and the well-rested and groomed Ovaro in the paddock, for Fargo had requested he not be stalled unless it rained. He threw on the blanket and pad, cinched the saddle, and slipped on the headstall.

"Looks like we're in it again, old warhorse," Fargo said as he slid the Henry into its boot and stepped up and over. "Keep your nose to the wind."

Avoiding town, holding his stallion to a trot, Fargo bore northeast from Tucson, heading toward the tiny Santa Cruz River. He felt safer out here in the open terrain, a landscape of sandy hills and flat expanses of desert covered with flowering mescal, white-plumed Spanish bayonet, and menacing prickly pear. Now and then, as Fargo etched the lay of the land in his memory, he let the Ovaro eat low-hanging mesquite pods.

Fargo's sense of safety, however, turned to hair-trigger alertness as he began to explore the river. Numerous sandbar willows provided good cover for ambushers. The cottonwoods lining both banks were budding into leaf, and although wind-twisted, could also conceal attackers. Fargo shucked out his Colt and kept his eyes to all sides.

Tall saguaros ringed Tucson, and Fargo gave each one a wide berth as he read the desert floor with a tracker's eye, looking for signs of Apaches and white men. The most dreaded deserts were in southwestern Arizona Territory, but Fargo preferred their vast emptiness to this south-central region with all its growth.

When trouble came, Fargo's frontier-honed eyes caught the subtle signs. He was riding the river again when he spotted, well out ahead, a flock of birds suddenly flying away from a shallow backwater of the river.

22

Fargo tugged rein.

"We're not close enough yet to scare those birds," Fargo muttered to his pinto. A moment later he spotted a glint of reflected light near the river.

Apaches, Fargo guessed. There were no horses hidden anywhere nearby, and Apaches were the only Southern Plains tribe that preferred to raid on foot. It was the Ovaro they were after, he figured, and not to ride—Apaches favored horse meat over most of the alternatives.

Fargo knew he would have to deal with the tribe before this new ordeal was over. But he had not survived in a dangerous land by foolishly riding into Apache traps. He wheeled the Ovaro around, splashed across to the opposite bank, and headed back toward town. The nights around here still had a snap to them, but by now the late-morning sun blazed hot as a branding iron under a cloudless blue sky.

Back in town, Fargo turned his horse over to the old Mexican, lugged his saddle to Amy's house, then headed across the plaza to look up Bearcat Lutz.

A saloon tout, a young man of mixed Indian and Mexican blood and skinny as a winter aspen, was out on the plaza steering visitors to his employer.

"El Oso Negro!" he shouted. "The Black Bear! Best saloon in town. Free lunch for liquor drinkers! Beautiful women in the rooms upstairs! You, friend!" he added, suddenly swerving toward Fargo and dipping his right hand into the front pocket of his white cotton trousers.

Quicker than thought, Fargo's Colt leaped into his fist.

"Madre de dios!" Slowly, the tout's hand emerged. It held a wooden token good for a free drink at the Black Bear.

"Sorry," Fargo told him. "I thought you were pulling down on me."

"Another hired killer kissing Bearcat's ass," the youth said, eyes taking Fargo's measure before the mixed-blood headed off.

"Go home and sleep it off," Fargo called after him. "You're drunk as Davy's saw."

The skinny kid turned unsteadily around. "Drunk? *Hombre*, I'm barreled, pickled, pie-eyed, shellacked, spifficated, jollified, stewed to the hat."

"Like I said—drunk."

"Drunk," he agreed, staggering away.

Fargo told himself to remember that face. The false alarm with the lippy kid embarrassed him into a more relaxed vigilance as he bisected the plaza. Near Lutz's house on the eastern edge of the plaza, a group of Mexican *braceros* were cleaning a statue and singing songs in Spanish while they worked. Each chorus ended with the long, falsetto *ay-y-y-y!*

Leery of all that cover, Fargo veered right, toward a group of horses and mules hitched to a tie-rail in front of the Sagebrush Saloon. When one of the horses shied, warning him, Fargo tucked and rolled just as a bullet whiffed past only inches from his head. He glimpsed a hulking figure hiding behind a big claybank's shoulder, then more shots sent adobe dust and chips into Fargo's eyes.

By the time he came up into a shooting crouch and had cleared his vision, Fargo had no target. Nor did he have proof—beyond the shooter's size—that Crawley Lake had just tried to kill him. But Fargo would find out one way or another, and he vowed that the moment he had proof, Lake was worm fodder.

"No duty to retreat," Fargo reminded himself as he aimed toward the oak-paneled front door of Bearcat Lutz's house.

4

"Beats bourbon and ditch water, eh, Fargo?" Lutz said, refilling Fargo's glass from a bottle of ten-year-old Scotch.

Fargo ignored the miner, more interested in the voluptuous young Mexican woman with the striking, nutshell-shaped eyes. She stood in the doorway of Lutz's library and kept flashing smiles at the new arrival, who was seated in front of Lutz's huge desk, from behind a graceful little fan of white net with gold sequins.

"Your wife?" Fargo asked.

Lutz stroked his silver goatee. "My wife? Hell no, I actually sleep with this one. Her name is Lupita, and she was selling it for nothing over at the Black Bear until I found her. As for my wife, that ice queen is a Boston Brahmin bitch who, thank God, has gone back east to tend to her sick mother. Which explains this saucy little Mexican tart in a thin cotton shift who is shamelessly throwing herself at you. Look, you can see her pussy hair through that shift."

"Yeah, I noticed," Fargo replied absently, still enjoying an eyeful.

"Friendly advice, Trailsman—leave this one alone. There's plenty more hot little senyoreeters in Tucson."

Fargo let the "advice" go, gazing around at the sumptuously appointed room. Books bound in scarlet morocco filled three walls, and the fourth was lined with lead candle sconces shaped like medieval beasts, and there was an expensive, uncovered harp with gilt strings that must have been pure hell to ship here safely. Gold-trimmed velvet curtains hung in the windows, and an interior patio, visible through a bank of windows, was bright with the plumage of exotic jungle birds.

"Will Crawley be at this meeting?" Fargo asked.

"Not a good idea. He'd rather shove a wolverine down his pants than work with you."

Lutz was a practiced liar, and Fargo couldn't tell if he knew about the attack out front or not. He guessed not. Lutz seemed eager to hire him—maybe too eager.

"Fargo," Lutz began after sending the girl away, "I take it you know William Bent and Ceran St. Vrain?"

Fargo nodded. "They built a trading post in the Texas Panhandle back in the thirties. Their post is still operating, last I heard."

"Oh, it is. You see, I worked there in the 1840s as a stock tender. One night I lit a shuck out of there with enough stolen gold to stake me to my own gambling hall in San Francisco. And I was able to parlay *that* into Lady Luck, the most productive silver mine in the Southwest. As you might imagine, I'm in no mood to give it up."

"Don't know's I blame you."

"But I *will* have to give it up if the goddamned Apaches succeed at scaring off the freighters. For one thing, I require a huge vat of cyanide for leaching the ore after it's been through the crusher, and that means constant resupply. But I've never faced redskins like Eskiminzin's bunch. Kiowa and Comanche are death to the devil, but an Apache, Christ! They'll cut your throat before you see them coming."

Fargo nodded. "I've never met another tribe that favors the night attack like Apaches do. I've never known a tribe to shoot better, either, or to be more merciless in battle."

"Brother, you're preaching to the choir. So far, they're still leery of entering Tucson proper because it's bristling with firearms. But you know it's open desert all around us, and the featherheads are raising hell with anyone who ventures into the outskirts—or tries to get into town."

Like the aspiring politico he was, Lutz began to warm to his own rhetoric. One fist beat the palm of his other hand to underscore his points.

"My silver mine is two miles north of town, and the Apaches are picking off my guards almost at will. Our Territorial Prison is near the mine, and I have a god-fear they mean to overrun it and free the prisoners."

"The Territorial Prison," Fargo cut in, "is at Fort Yuma."

"Well, we needed one here, so I started it. And just in case Amy Hanchon has filled your gourd with her whining about her old man, it's not just my interest that's at stake here. Tucson has not quite four hundred permanent settlers yet, but a constant flood of visitors drives up the spending—*if* the red Arabs don't dry it up. And the latest U.S. marshals' report claims that Indian raids in this region have cost a half-million head of sheep and cattle in the past four years alone."

Which hardly made up, Fargo figured, for the millions of buffalo white men were already beginning to slaughter just for sport, or the Indians' sacred mountains blown to smithereens just to root for gold. Fargo's skin felt slimy simply being here. Men like Bearcat Lutz knew hundreds of people, but hadn't one true friend. In the world he chose to inhabit, friendship was as rare as mercy.

"And do you know why, Fargo?" Lutz steamed on, his wellgroomed face a mask of indignation. "It's calamity howlers like Daniel Hanchon who bring law and government in, ruining the bonanza for everybody. But Bearcat Lutz was smart enough to work his entire mining operation out on the back of an envelope, and I'm smart enough to kill any swinging dick who fights me."

Shrewdness seeped into Lutz's steel gray eyes. "I know you're poking Hanchon's daughter, and who can blame you? I mean to tap that stuff myself. But, Fargo, I hope you've got more brains than to try and help her old man."

Fargo sipped the Scotch, which seemed like flavored water compared to typical frontier mash. "The crap you might hear about me is folk legend, the usual Robin Hood hogwash. Daniel Hanchon never bought me a beer. I'm a paid jobber, and his daughter has no money to pay me."

"If that's true, I've got plenty of work for you. The U.S. government is filled with Indian lovers, but why should we palefaces get the crappy end of the stick? I've got enough on my plate as it is. There's serious talk of severing New Mexico from the Arizona Territory, and when that happens the current governor will be assigned to Santa Fe, opening up the governorship out here. Naturally, since I'll control Arizona by then, I intend to fill that opening, but it means plenty of politicking."

Lutz paused and flipped open a humidor, removing two cigars while he studied Fargo thoughtfully. "Fargo," he said, handing him a cigar and match, "do you mind my asking what was your last paying job?"

Fargo bit the end off his stogie and struck the match to life on his boot, firing up the cigar. "Nothing to brag about. I took a job as a guard for a merchant's caravan from Santa Fe to Durango, Mexico, along the Santa Fe Trail."

"All right, that's good, honest work. But, Fargo, a smart man like you can't be earning just enough to keep the wolf from the door."

Lutz turned a territorial map so Fargo could see it. "All through here," he said, indicating a wide swath between San Carlos Lake to the north and the border with Mexico to the south, "Comanche, Kiowa, and especially Apaches are marauding with impunity. They hit stage stations, ranches, mail riders, then disappear into the landscape."

Fargo listened, but also kept his eyes on all those windows. Crawley was out there somewhere, seething mad after being forced to crawfish last night in front of his boss.

"I don't need to worry about Chief Red Sleeves, leader of the Mimbrenos Apaches," Lutz continued, "because they're staying in the Dragoon Mountains and choose to fight Mexicans. The Messy Apaches do raid, but they always move on. It's only Eskiminzin's group that needs . . . dealing with."

Lutz paused to keep his cigar glowing. "I gave the job to Crawley and told him piecework wouldn't get it done. He took my meaning, all right, and hired over two hundred Papago and Mexican mercenaries to wipe out Eskiminzin's camp—only about one hundred fifty Apaches. We found half the mercenaries with their skulls crushed and their castrated manhood crammed into their mouths. Not surprisingly, Crawley is now convinced it's a fool's errand to exterminate Indians."

"Nobody's permanent," Fargo remarked quietly, eliciting an approving grin from Lutz.

"*That's* the spirit, stout lad. You know, I chased all the garlics and their 'Spanish seal' land-grant claims out of here just by killing two of them. Sadly, the Holy Roman Church and their mealymouth psalm-singers are pushing this 'red men have souls' business. Fargo, to hell with the bench of bishops. I've noticed how, ever since Crawley sent that nun to Jesus, the local church has gone back to saving souls instead of meddling in business affairs."

Lutz opened the top drawer of his desk and removed a chamois pouch. He opened the drawstring and big silver pesos bounced onto the desk.

"These spend everywhere between the border and the Oro Valley, north of us. I'm putting you on the payroll at five dollars a day. There's fifty dollars in this pouch—we'll call it an advance. Are you with me?"

"A U.S. marshal earns a dollar a day," Fargo replied. "Hell yes, I'm in."

Lutz extended a hand and Fargo shook it, feeling like he was buried up to his neck in a snake pit.

"As to my actual plan," Lutz added, "I'm still tinkering with it. You'll be the first to know when it's ready. But, believe me, this time it won't be 'piecework.' We'll get rid of that Apache bunch once and for all."

Fargo emerged carefully onto the central plaza, his eyes everywhere at once in the bustling midday activity. Crawley Lake was still unaccounted for, and Fargo had deliberately humiliated him yesterday to force a clash. Lutz was the head of the snake, all right, but Crawley was the fangs.

Fargo knew damn good and well how things stood when an outsider—especially one with a "reputation" he never wanted— rode into a wide-open settlement like Tucson. Somebody had to test his mettle publicly, and if the outlander prevailed, he was left alone. Some of Lutz's thugs saw the killing on the plaza yesterday, but not enough—and not close up. It seemed logical to start at the saloon near Lutz's house, which seemed to draw regulators like flies to syrup.

Fargo didn't like playing it this way. "Never draw attention to yourself" was one of his instinctive rules during danger. Live in the shadows. Hide by day and become a creature of the night. But some dire situations required a man to send in his card.

He glanced up at a wood sign with gilded letters spelling out SAGEBRUSH SALOON. But the sign was the only thing fancy about the adobe hovel. The front door was an open archway, and he spotted a raw plank bar supported by trestles. Most of the customers sat around on old vegetable cans, using everything from coffins to egg crates as tables.

"Oye! Listen, hired gun, that's your kind of watering hole. Plenty of killers."

Fargo spotted the skinny saloon tout he'd seen earlier, a youth barely twenty or so of mixed Mexican and Indian blood. He wore tapered cotton pants, tied in front with tabs, rope sandals, and a straw Sonora hat. He was shirtless, revealing a body so scrawny the ribs looked like barrel staves.

"That mouth of yours could get dangerous to your health," Fargo warned him. "I thought you touted for the Black Bear?"

"That's me, good for all the squaw work. But last year I was a trapper of long-fur pelts. Made a fortune. I even mixed my own scents."

Fargo forced back a grin at the kid's blustery, boastful manner. "Friend, if you did, you were behind times. The long-fur pelts were taken twenty, twenty-five years ago."

"Hijo! Son of God, don't you think I figured that out? You dime-a-death killers are even stupider than God made you."

"Oh, I've killed, all right, but killing ain't always murder," Fargo told him.

"Chinga tu madre," the tout spat in a truculent voice.

"I didn't bring *your* mother into this," Fargo protested.

"Vaya! With my own eyes I saw you leave Bearcat's house just now."

"So what? Don't get your bowels in an uproar, appearances can be deceiving. You heard about the vigilante killed at San Antonio church yesterday?"

The kid grinned. "They say it was the fall that killed him. Too bad, did you lose a friend?"

"Not hardly. I'm the jasper who killed him."

The tout paled a few shades. "Jesus Christ and various saints! Buckskins, tall, brown face lace . . . hell, you *are* Skye Fargo. I call me Snakeroot. So how's it come that the Trailsman can leave Bearcat's house alive?"

"Snakeroot, huh?" Fargo repeated the name in a dubious tone. "Before I say anything more, how do you feel about Lutz? On the level."

"You want it on the level? I'd kiss the devil's ass in hell for a chance to rip Bearcat open from neck to nuts. I never trust any man who shows too many teeth when he smiles. Hell, I know plenty about that son of a bitch. Before he started hiring out his killing, I once watched him beat an old man to death with a pick handle."

The mixed-blood hiked up his right pant's leg to reveal an iron-and-brass Spanish dag in a leather sheath. "*Lo juro.* I swear it, someday I will irrigate his guts."

Fargo knuckled his hand aside, letting the pants leg cover the knife again. "We all need reminding more than instructing. Don't be flashing that blade, old son. I'd guess you're a mix of Mexican and Apache blood. You know it's a prison offense under territorial law for a mestizo to carry a weapon."

Snakeroot looked smug. "You can read bloodlines, but most of these town gringos think I had a white father and Mexican mother. They still don't like me, but I have many rights of the white man."

Fargo nodded toward the Sagebrush. "Including the right to drink in saloons?"

Snakeroot made a face. "I like tiswin," he said, meaning Apache corn beer. "They don't sell it here. The whiskey here is burro piss, but the tequila is the best made north of Nogales."

"What's that empty building next to the saloon?" Fargo asked as the two men approached the open doorway of the Sagebrush.

"*Was* a dancehall. They had so many killings and fights they boarded up the windows. Say, Fargo?"

"Yeah?"

"If you just killed a strangler yesterday, this hole is the last place you want to be seen." Snakeroot hummed the "Funeral March" to make his point.

Fargo grinned. "There's always a chance they'll miss me and hit you."

The saloon was thick with a pall of smoke and reeked of unwashed masculinity. As soon as Fargo's tall, imposing figure filled the archway, conversation ceased.

With a practiced eye, Fargo sought out the potential trouble-makers. Besides their sawed-off express guns, most of the vigilantes favored sturdy trousers of bleached canvas—their "uniforms." Not every customer was a hard case—he spotted several men wearing range clothes and neckerchiefs, some of the first white ranchers in the Territory. But that scowling lummox standing poker rigid at the end of the bar, staring daggers at Fargo, looked like trouble.

"That's Kinch McKinney," Snakeroot muttered. "Meaner than a badger in a barrel. *Cuidado.*"

"I'm always careful," Fargo replied.

"Welcome to Tucson, Mr. Fargo, it's a pleasure to have you here," a bald-headed barkeep blandished like a rented toady.

"Thank you, bottles. I expect you'll be pleased when I leave, too."

"That's an open question right now, Mr. Fargo. Name your poison."

Fargo ordered tequila served with salt and lime.

"A quiet life and a long one," Snakeroot toasted after it was served.

Fargo couldn't help a stab of irony at the toast. The "quiet" part had already passed him by, and the "long" part hardly seemed likely.

"Hey, Lanny!" Kinch McKinney bellowed at the barkeep in a self-satisfied voice that instantly irked Fargo. "I don't care if you serve that skinny 'breed, but serving a sheep-humping, barn-burning, back-shooting shit-heel is going too damn far."

Fargo, now that the test he sought was starting, made a placatory gesture with his hands. "Hold your powder, boys. I'm on the payroll with you now."

McKinney stared at him with angry eyes like molten ore. "So goddamn what, drifter," he roweled, voice yielding even more to his ire. "What do you want, a blue ribbon from God?"

"Pack it in, Kinch," the bartender warned. "This hombre knows 'b' from a bull's foot."

McKinney's double ten lay across the plank bar, and Fargo kept it in view as he ordered two mugs of beer. In Tucson beer was kept cold on winter ice harvested in the mountains, and Fargo carried the sweat-beaded mugs to a packing-crate table. Snakeroot, watching the Trailsman from curious eyes, pulled a meerschaum pipe from his pocket and stuffed it with coarse black shag.

"It don't add up, Fargo," he finally said, "and that's the swear-to-God truth. No matter how you cipher it."

"Cipher what?"

"You. Noble crusader Skye Fargo working for the Bearcat."

"Maybe I'm *not* working for him," Fargo suggested. "Maybe I'm just here to get a scent."

"You mean a stench. Like this." Snakeroot pulled on his pipe

32

until it was simmering. The strong Mexican tobacco smelled like hides being branded.

Fargo ignored this sideshow. "Look, I know you speak Spanish. Can you palaver in Apache, too?"

The mixed-blood's face suddenly shut like a vault door. "Why?"

"It's a skill I might need. My own Apache is limited."

"I'm pretty good, but my mother taught me, and she was a Messy—you know, Mescalero. Aravaipa ain't too different. But, Fargo, Eskiminzin is a good man to let alone."

Fargo felt plenty of eyes on him, but kept his attention on Kinch McKinney, who was downing shots to fortify himself for a play against Fargo.

"Either I make medicine with Eskiminzin," Fargo replied, "or there's a good chance his entire clan circle will be wiped out. Which also leaves me shit out of luck for allies against the stranglers."

"Wiped out?"

Fargo nodded.

"*Hijo!* But Lutz has been trying to do that for years."

"I know, but he seems confident he can do it this time. Snakeroot, can you ride?"

The mixed-blood nodded. "Like a Comanche. In Mexico I was a *jinete*, a horse-breaker, for two years. Then I started to cough up blood and had to quit."

"You're a cockchafer, Fargo!" McKinney shouted from the bar. "You gonna marry that skinny little greaser gal-boy? Sittin' there talkin' lovey like newlyweds, *shit*! These two prefer the pole over the hole."

"Rein it in," Fargo snapped when Snakeroot, face twisted with rage, made a move toward his knife. "You pull that frog-sticker, and they'll shoot both of us to streamers."

Snakeroot shook his head. "*Mira!* Look, Fargo, I'd put Tucson behind me in a puffin' hurry. You're going to get your tail in a crack."

"It's already in a crack, as usual. Never mind. Tell me, are the Aravaipa still north of Green Valley?"

"Nah, pony soldiers ran them out. Now they're squatting in an abandoned Mexican pueblo halfway between here and Colossal Cave. They scratch by with raiding and working as mules for *contrabandistas*."

Fargo glanced around, wondering where the hell Crawley Lake was. The man may have backed down yesterday, but that didn't mean he was all bluff and bluster. The only thing Crawley was afraid to do was die. All else was fair game.

"Quick," he told Snakeroot, "let's spit on the deal. Will you work for me?"

"Look, Fargo, you being a big man and all don't cut no ice with me. I don't live in any man's pocket."

"No one's asking you to," Fargo said impatiently, though he recognized something of himself in this lad's fierce independence. "I'll pay three dollars a day."

"Hell, I'm in." Both men spit on their palms and shook hands. "But sailing under false colors around here, *if* that's what you're up to, is a sure trip to the bone orchard. We—"

"Here it comes," Fargo cut him off, watching McKinney push away from the bar. "Get back, Snakeroot, and sing out if a shooter gets behind me."

The moment McKinney snatched up his express gun, Fargo jerked his Colt. The sound, when he cocked it, arrested McKinney's motion.

"Well, ain't *you* the bravo? Leave that smoke pole on the bar," Fargo ordered in a take-charge manner, "or I'll drill one into your lights. We'll settle this with short irons."

The crowd wasn't sure if that was a brief smile or just a predatory twitch of Fargo's lips. McKinney, three sheets to the wind, tossed his crowd-leveler down and took a few steps toward Fargo as the latter leathered his six-gun.

"All right, buckskin, skin it back."

"I generally don't waste a good bullet on a shit-eating coward," Fargo told him, talking in a tone used with children. "I just kill your type with a rock."

A new surge of anger tightened McKinney's lips and face. "That just flat out does it, Fargo. Now you'll grin in hell!"

Fargo's gut wanted to kill this lump of vermin and do the world a favor. But he had already killed one strangler, and he didn't need a well-armed mob like this motivated to kill him on sight. McKinney was still clearing leather when Fargo snapped off a .36 caliber round, planting it precisely between the second and third knuckle of McKinney's right hand—and, thus, ripping apart a major tendon responsible for flexing the fingers, a tendon that would never heal well.

McKinney dropped his gun and yowled like a cat with a torn claw. His eyes lost their focus as pain blurred them.

"He's ruint my *hand*!" he screamed.

Fargo cocked the Colt again, and McKinney shut up. "You're taking up too much of my air," Fargo said coldly. "Now get the hell out of here, or my next bullet will ruin your pump."

5

The bell of San Antonio rang once, one p.m. and the middle of siesta. The central plaza was almost deserted when Fargo parted from Snakeroot, returned to Amy Hanchon's house, and thumped on the front door. He heard the cover on the Judas hole squeak back, then a stifled exclamation. A moment later the door swung inward.

"Skye! Thank God you're all right! *Are* you all right?"

"Spry and chipper as ever," he assured her.

"Come in and eat something."

Fargo's saddle lay behind the door. He bent to pull the cleaning kit from a saddle pocket and then sat in a chair with a good view out the front window, running a wiping patch down the bore of his Colt and placing a drop of gun oil on the pivot screw.

"How did your 'meeting' with Lutz go?" Amy asked him, returning from the kitchen with a steaming plate of carne asada. She cast a glance at his six-gun but said nothing.

Fargo tied into his food before he spoke. "The whole thing was moonshine. Old Bearcat is pure cheapjack, and you can't trust a word he says."

A skeptical dimple wrinkled her right cheek. "Skye, I already told you all that. What else did you learn? Did you—?"

Fargo laughed, raising a hand to silence her. "Turn off the tap, lass. I'm just easing into it, all right?"

She blushed—about the same shade, Fargo noticed with amusement, as the immaculate, apple-blossom pink gloves she wore.

"I'm sorry, Skye. I'm all wrought up. Since father was seized, I can discipline everything except my emotions. They refuse to be curbed by reason or even fatigue. Only . . . only the pleasure I shared with you last night took my mind off everything. Shall we return to my bed for more of the same? Right now?"

Two things Fargo truly hated were shooting a horse and refusing a beautiful woman. But even though Amy's words sparked a warm stirring below his belt, a glance out the window settled the issue.

"Best offer I've had all year," Fargo finally answered. "But we best delay it."

"Oh, don't be an old sobersides."

"I'm not. Take a look out front."

She did, and saw slab-faced Crawley Lake and three of his minions standing about twenty feet in front of the house. Even from his chair Fargo could see that Crawley's eyes blazed with malice.

"Skye! What happened to cause this?"

"Ah, it was pee doodles. Just a little gunplay in the Sagebrush."

"With Crawley?"

"Crawley," Fargo replied, "is brave when the odds are with him, but isn't too eager to pull down on me in a fair fight. I'm sure, though, he tried to murder me this morning on the plaza. He's just playing the he-bear out there now."

"Well, if it's all 'pee doodles,'" she snapped, "may I ask you to skip the twaddle and buncombe and tell me if you've learned anything about irrelevant things like my father?"

Fargo swallowed, loading up his fork again. "Not really," he admitted. "There was no good time to bring him up. Lutz is all fired up on some scheme to wipe out the local Apaches, and I let him talk because I can't let that happen."

"No good time . . . ?" She aimed a defiant stare at him, angry green eyes sparkling. "You gave me to understand that you were working to free my father—not to help the murdering Apaches."

"Don't be a simp. I know those Apaches would skin me out like they would a rabbit. But if Lutz manages to make good on his threat, there'll be Indian uprisings from El Paso to the Snake River. White settlers here in Arizona are already on the feather edge of extinction."

Fargo finished eating and pushed his plate away. "Besides, to hear you take on about it, the only Hanchon in danger is your father. What about you, m'love? You can't just bust him out and go about your business. They'll kill both of you. No, the whole shootin' match has to come down."

The grim truth of his words battered down her defenses. Her angry certainty abruptly cracked, then crumbled completely as tears welled from her eyes.

"You believe that can be done?" she asked him.

"To the marrow of my bones," Fargo assured her. "It's damn long odds, but Lutz can be stopped and your father sprung. They all foul their nests sooner or later."

A mechanical smile was the best she could muster. "So he never even mentioned my father? Is he still alive?"

"He's still alive, but Amy, look at this thing close. I can't pretend to work for Bearcat while pumping him about your father. Lutz doesn't trust me as it is. But just calm down. I'm riding out to the mine today to see if I can spot your father. By the way, have you got a good likeness of him?"

"Of course. But you're riding out today—in broad daylight? To quote my father, that would make even a mule think twice."

"I've tangled with Apaches after dark. I like the daylight odds better."

"Skye, I'm so grateful that you're helping. But *how* can you possibly take on so many killers?"

"Soft beds make soft soldiers," Fargo assured her. "Numbers aren't the whole story here. These town ruffians are dough bellies who go puny in the back country. That's where I'll fight 'em."

"But . . . by yourself?"

"Maybe not," Fargo said mysteriously, glancing out the windows. "Looks like Crawley moved on. I best get thrashing."

"Skye?"

"Yeah?"

"One of the guards out at Lutz's mine is especially dangerous—Hachita, Spanish for hatchet. The man is a notorious brute and hopelessly insane."

"Just proves I'm a blessed man," Fargo quipped. "Why'n'cha toss in a plague of locusts, too?"

"Where will you sleep tonight?" she asked.

"Same place I usually sleep—under the stars."

"Don't be silly. There's an old posada near—"

"No lodging houses," Fargo interrupted. "I'll sleep where they can't trap me."

"Will you think about what we did in bed?"

"I'll do more than think about it," Fargo assured her.

"What does that mean—*oh*!" She blushed as she caught his drift.

Fargo laughed. "That shocks you?"

"No. It's exciting. Maybe I'll try it, too."

At the door Fargo hefted his saddle onto his right shoulder. Amy, smelling like lavender and honeysuckle, leaned into him and ran her fingers through his beard.

"Tough as bore bristles," she marveled, next sliding her hands over his sloping pectorals. "Mm . . . you're a hard man, Skye Fargo. Hard as sacked salt."

"And getting harder," he assured her.

"And we're just going to waste it?"

"Nope," he said, lifting the bar off the door, "we're just gonna let it simmer a bit longer, then we'll really turn the heat up."

Outside on the plaza, Fargo stuck to the shadows and kept his attention everywhere, especially up on the roofs. Even in town he used his eyes the same way he did on the open trail—he kept his focus relaxed at the middle range and let everything "come up to his eye."

Fargo spotted the Ovaro the moment he turned onto the dirt surface of Silver Street. He watched the black-and-white stallion, drunk on spring, run hard in the big paddock as he worked out the night kinks, his quarters sinking with the power and lengthening of his stride.

Fargo found the old hostler in the tackroom, switching Fargo's northern-range stirrups for a pair of tapaderos or box stirrups, widely used among desert riders to protect their feet and ankles in dangerous cactus country.

"You need these on your saddle," the old man said. "It is all desert around us, sharp desert."

Fargo thanked him. A tall prickly pear had grazed him yesterday, his thick buckskins barely protecting him.

"Senor," he said, holding out an Indian parfleche and two bits, "favor of parched corn?"

"Of course." The old man filled the bag from a bin behind him. Parched corn was no feast, but Fargo favored it for jobs like this one because it was filling and both horse and rider could eat it.

Fargo tacked the Ovaro, loosened the Henry in its boot, then forked leather and reined around to the north. Homes gave way quickly to crop fields, some of which were protected from animals and wind by the imported osage orange tree, which made a hedge of wicked thorns.

The mine was only two miles outside of Tucson, in the parched foothills of a bleak, sterile mountain range. Fargo knew, from his earlier scout, that a deep-rutted freight road led to it through the dusty sagebrush, but he avoided the road and reluctantly bore left into the cover of tall saguaros—cover for him but also for ambushers.

Fargo rode up out of the valley surrounding Tucson, his eyes in constant motion. He cast a quick backward glance and, through the shimmering heat ripples, the motley sprawl of town looked unreal, like painted flats at the rear of a theater stage.

"A bunch of damn flies buzzing around a molasses barrel," he told the Ovaro, who nickered in apparent agreement.

Fargo was surprised to find, at the border of fertile valley and sandy desert, a rude shanty and a scratch-penny herd of about a dozen longhorns, one of only a few left in a time of increasing Indian raids and decreasing government control. To the southwest tribes, white man's cattle was "slow elk," free for the taking.

The Trailsman's eye watched for sign made by horsemen or Apaches on foot, but constant blow sand around here obscured trails quickly—an advantage to any Apaches watching him, and Fargo assumed some were. The game trace he was following dipped into a series of low washes ahead, potential death traps, and instead Fargo reined toward a narrow divide between two small valleys.

He also avoided the temptation to ride through numerous gullies washed red with eroded soil. Their sandy bottoms made for easy and quiet riding, but Apaches usually attacked on foot and preferred narrow traps. Two miles as the crow flies became a torturous route for Fargo as he waged the struggle for survival. At times he drifted near the freight road, and once he heard iron rims scraping the hardpan.

About halfway between Tucson and the foothills, Fargo hobbled his stallion and climbed up onto the crown of a huge boulder, taking a long squint around, looking for movement, reflections, dust puffs. Despite all his caution and savvy, however, only a few minutes later he almost rode into the belly of a cunning beast.

He had just skirted a small brush canyon, forcing him briefly onto a slice of desert that was scant cover, mostly a mix of sagebrush grass and salt-desert shrub. Abruptly, the Ovaro's ears pricked forward as the experienced horse recognized the Indian smell, alerting as Fargo had taught him to.

40

Fargo glimpsed a face under a red headband, peeking from behind a saguaro, and realized it was root hog or die. He reined in hard, popped off three rounds from his Colt to keep them honest, then wheeled his wide-eyed horse.

"*Go*, you son of thunder, hee-*yah*!"

Sensing the danger the Ovaro bolted like shot from a cannon. Fargo, still not used to the tapaderos, lost both stirrups but managed to cling to the horn while he bounced on top of the saddle like a rag doll. Rifle shots cracked behind him, several of the bullets snapping close to his ear, snapping loud and making his heart gallop. Arrows *fwipped* past, one so close the eagle-feather fletching tickled his neck.

As usual with Apaches, Fargo had seen almost nothing of them. He fled due west, jogged north, then cut due east again, able now to see the Lady Luck mine amidst ugly scars and scabs from exploration pits in the terrain. Fargo knew the Apaches might have divided up into smaller groups, a favorite trick. Nor dare he ride in closer with guards watching him from the mine.

There was only one way in—on foot, beating white man and Apache alike at their own game.

"Hey, holy man! You better put your shoulder into that motherlovin' cart, or I'll whip you till your asshole bleeds!"

Reverend Daniel Hanchon was pouring sweat, but the arid desert air sponged it up the moment it appeared, denying him the solace of a cool breeze. He strained to push a cart filled with ore tailings along a narrow-gauge track.

"Please," he begged a guard who held a long blaksnake whip, "just a little more water."

"Happy to oblige, dad," Hamp Johnson replied, fumbling open the fly of his canvas trousers and urinating on a cringing Hanchon's legs. "Drink *that*, you whining she-male. Fresh-made lemonade— you know, the drink they *all* want in hell."

"Hell?" the exhausted preacher repeated. "I'm afraid even hell would spit you back up, Johnson."

"Apple-polishing don't work on me, bible-thumper," Johnson replied sarcastically. He was a big, flabby-faced Texan wearing leather boots with the star of Texas worked into the tops. "But just for them kind words, here's a little kiss for you."

The long whip cracked, the stone-embedded popper licked at his ribs with a barbed tongue, and Hanchon hissed in pain.

Hamp Johnson stalked closer, his piggish eyes lethal. "Now, you lily-livered cheese dick, you *will* work harder or I'll strip you down buck, stake you out, and pour honey on you. Then I'll watch red ants eat you down to the bone. Oh, you ain't *heard* screamin' till you hear that, no sir."

"You won't kill me," Hanchon shot back defiantly, half hoping they would. "Too many men who can put you in prison now know I'm here. They won't buy the phony rape charge Bearcat is peddling."

"Oh, your pedestal is high, is it? Holy man, you are so full of shit your feet are sliding. Let's play pretend games and say you really are some big muckety-muck, too important for a ruffian like me to murder. But plenty of guilty men choose to pull their own plugs, am I right? Hell, glom that slope right behind you. That's a forty-degree talus slope, looser than a whippoorwill's bowels. A man could easy jump to his death. Most especial, what they call a 'remorseful preacher' that raped an innocent girl like Lupita."

Hanchon could bear no more and groaned at the effort as he pushed the heavy cart into motion again. The whip cracked behind him, and more fire licked at the back of his thighs.

"Maybe you need an easier job," Johnson shouted behind him. "Maybe on the honey wagon, emptying shit pots. Take a look up toward the assay shack."

Hanchon did, and recognized a man with a face so evil that Hanchon could not look at it longer than a few seconds at a time. When he turned away now, disgusted, Johnson shook with laughter.

"'At's right, preacher man—Hachita. Now, you slack off on me, I'll likely just beat you half-haywire. But Hachita? Nobody reins in *that* crazy bastard. He'll slice you open from scalp to toenails and eat your liver while you watch."

6

Fargo found a rocky seam, swung down, and led the Ovaro into cover, then quickly watered the stallion from his hat before feeding him a few handfuls of parched corn. Before he hobbled the pinto foreleg to rear with rawhide strips, Fargo examined each hoof for cracks, thorns, and stone bruises. He wanted no nasty surprises if a fast getaway was needed.

This final leg, crossing several hundred yards of scant-grown, upward-sloping terrain, would test all of Fargo's skills at movement and concealment. Plenty of eyes would be searching, and Fargo took comfort in the color of his faded buckskins, which blended well with sandy terrain.

Fargo blackened his face with gunpowder to cut down reflection. He reluctantly left his Henry in its boot and even draped his gun belt over the saddle horn, leaving his Colt. His only weapon would be the knife in his boot, but Fargo figured if he was spotted he'd be shot to trap bait before he could pull it. So the key was not to be spotted.

He ducked out of the rock seam and rolled into a little depression, a merciless desert sun baking him while he got a good size-up of the Lady Luck and surroundings. Fargo dare not use binoculars this close for fear of reflections, but his distance-trained eyes took in plenty. A rocky plateau rose above and behind the mine and held what had to be the prison, a mud-brick building surrounded by a palisade of sharpened stakes. Flowing straight down toward him was a long talus slope, which formed a wide fan at its base.

Large piles of ore tailings marked each productive mine shaft, and an assay shack stood near the head-frame of the main shaft. Fargo decided to aim toward an open-faced shed near the biggest pile of ore tailings. He counted at least ten armed guards, but none near the shed.

Fargo moved at a low crawl, eyes constantly searching for swales, knolls, hummocks, anything to keep him below the horizon line. He knew that no terrain was ever truly level, and by laying his head down on the ground he could pick out the tiny depressions. Fargo soldiered on doggedly, climbing the steep backside of the ridge.

By the time his elbows and toes were scraped raw, Fargo was close enough to clearly make out the "prisoners" (he considered them slaves), a tatterdemalion lot whose clothing was mostly filthy rag streamers. The most emaciated of the bunch wore nothing but grain-sack trousers. Fargo searched every face, but failed to spot any resembling the portrait of Daniel Hanchon that Amy had shown him.

Maybe he was already dead, Fargo fretted, wondering how to tell Amy.

Fargo finally rolled fast into the open-faced shed and took cover behind a stack of supporting timbers just in the nick of time. A Mexican guard with a scarred and pitted face, and dark eyes like pools of acid, emerged from the assay shack. He stared toward the narrow-gauge track and an old man, much older than Hanchon, with skin the color of faded parchment. The oldster had collapsed beside a car of ore tailings, scrawny chest heaving in a way that told Fargo it was the end.

"*Mira!*" the guard called to another thug nearby. "Look, Hamp! A gutless old man blocks the tracks like a dead horse. Let's help him move."

That was Hachita, Fargo realized when he saw the infamous bone-handle hatchet in the murderer's sash. Hachita moved closer, uncoiling his blacksnake. A second, flabby-faced guard in Texas boots looked on, grinning with anticipation.

"*Vamanos, viejo!*" Hachita barked, cracking his whip. "Let's go, old fart, you are no longer a mine owner. *Manos a la obra!* Get to work!"

The old man made it up to one bloody knee, then collapsed again.

"*Ay!* This lout of a prisoner is a rebel, eh? *Here* is what we dish up to rebels, *pendejo.*"

Fargo was forced to watch the unspeakable act with a sense of growing horror. Showing a serene mastery of his bloody craft, knowing the other prisoners were watching, Hachita murdered the old man in cold blood as an example, his singing whip shredding him to bloody tatters in blow after stinging, slicing blow.

Anger rose within Fargo, sudden as a squall. But he knew that blind anger got a man killed fast, so he simply snuffed it out.

"Today," Hachita announced grandly, "the buzzards feast."

His flat voice, Fargo realized, never varied in pitch or tone—the way he imagined a dead man might sound if he could suddenly speak after centuries of silence.

"Corpse detail!" the man called Hamp shouted. "Drag this worm castle down the slope where we won't have to smell it."

Fargo's face was suddenly alert as he spotted Daniel Hanchon wrestling his ore car toward the nearby pile of tailings. They had to be piled up to clear the shafts, and when the mine played out, local Mexicans would sift through them for bits of silver the miners ignored.

"Lookit there, holy man!" shouted Hamp. "Another prisoner has cashed in his own chips. Must be the burden of his guilt. Lotsa that goin' round."

"See how it is?" Hachita's lifeless voice added. "Around here, soul saver, people take sick, all of a sudden like. *A ver!* Let's see if you can stay healthy, eh?"

Both guards moved on up the slope, sharing a bottle of whiskey as they hazed and occasionally whipped other workers. Fargo waited until Hanchon was only ten feet in front of the shed.

"*Psst!* Rev! Reverend Hachon! Over here!"

Fargo moved as close to the open front as he dared. Startled, Hanchon glanced in his direction, sun-strained eyes squinting as they took his measure. The man was in his middle forties with silver hair sweat-plastered to his head like a helmet.

"My name is Skye Fargo. Your daughter hired me. I'm going to try to help you."

"Skye—of course, the Trailsman. God bless you, son. Just tell my daughter to go back east. I admire your courage, but it would require Camp Grant soldiers to smash Lutz's operation, and the leadership there are on his payroll. Besides, the camp barely has enough troopers to protect their garrison. Lutz is cunning—he waited for the turmoil back east to siphon off more soldiers before he made his move."

"No man who wants to survive out here can ever view soldiers as his only hope. When there's trouble, I'm not one to settle for washing bricks," Fargo assured him. "I've got an idea baking. Right now it's only half-baked, but it's hope."

"Even if I escape, son, there's a trumped-up rape charge hanging over me. There was never even a writ of capias, a warrant for arrest. But the woman who accused me is popular in Tucson, Bearcat's consort. A woman's word is unassailable in Western courts."

"There's a sure way," Fargo gainsaid. "We get her to recant her testimony in writing."

"I believe in miracles, Mr. Fargo, but short of heavenly intervention, Lupita will never do that. Not when she's Bearcat's mistress."

Fargo couldn't deny the mistress part, but so what? Nobody missed a slice off a cut loaf, and besides, that smoldering, groin-tickling glance she gave him earlier at Lutz's house was familiar to Fargo—none of which bore repeating to a minister.

Hanchon glanced toward the crumpled, bloody body up the slope. "There lies Rafe Conlin, may God have mercy on his soul."

"Amen," Fargo said. "But Hachita showed damn little mercy to his body."

"Oh, that was routine." Hanchon tipped his head in the direction of the retreating guards. "That Hachita is Satan incarnate, Mr. Fargo, and Hamp Johnson is his hellish understudy. Killing and maiming unarmed, defenseless men seems to leave them blissful."

"You rate them too high a danger," Fargo insisted. "Don't get fact mixed up with stupid. That kind of thinking makes a man give up too soon."

"You don't understand. These aren't just vigilantes putting the noose before the gavel—they are fabricating the crimes and paying a hanging judge to make it 'legal.' It's all just a front for Lutz's slave gang."

"I already figured as much, and it changes nothing. Comes a time in every man's life when he has to fight or show yellow. We can bring this whole shebang down if we play it foxy."

Fargo's words didn't seem to register. Hanchon's shoulders slumped under the weight of emotional defeat. "Pride comes straight from hell, and that devil Lutz *is* proud. I always told Amy, a stout back and a hopeful spirit—that's what will win the West. Well, I'm losing both."

Fargo could see that Hanchon was on the verge of giving up. Nor could he blame him. Even if soldiers were available, with Apaches controlling most of the territory outside Tucson, the fifty-five-mile ride to Camp Grant to alert them would be a forlorn hope. And while there was much talk of a transcontinental telegraph coming soon, Tucson remained completely cut off because local lines were always torn down.

"I'm not a religious man," Fargo said. "But I've always admired a good believer. A preacher I met in St. Joe, he told me God would help any man, but only after he stood on his own two feet like a man. You've got a lovely daughter fighting like hell for you, don't give up on her."

Hanchon weighed the words, then nodded. "Amy. Will you protect her, Mr. Fargo?"

"I'll do my damndest and then some. You have to get back to work, and I have to skedaddle out of here. First, though, I've got a few questions about this hellhole, starting with where the guards stay."

Fargo finished making a mind map of the Lady Luck, then essayed the dangerous journey back to his hidden horse, under a bright sun, without being spotted.

He made it back to the rocky seam without incident, but from the moment Fargo hit leather and wheeled the Ovaro south, he felt a familiar warning. It was not a specific fear, only an odd, premonitory heaviness concentrated on his nape.

"It won't be long, old campaigner, we're gonna have heel flies on our trail," he remarked to his mount. "Get set to stretch it out."

Halfway back to Tucson, Fargo's hunch panned out. A half-dozen riders, hiding in a parched creek bed, fanned out onto the hot sand behind him, ki-yiing their horses to a gallop and hurling lead at their quarry.

Fargo's best defense, in a run-down, was his superior stallion, who had once won a grueling, all-day race in the salt desert of Utah. Now, even before Fargo slapped the reins on his neck, the Ovaro had bolted off with the devil on his tail. Sage and creosote and prickly pear rolled past in a blur as hot slugs thickened the air around Fargo and forced him to lean low in the saddle.

The Trailsman recognized Crawley Lake leading the pack on a big blood bay. Then it occurred to Fargo: Crawley had played this brilliantly. Fargo was being "funneled" between two steep dropoffs. The only possible escape lay dead ahead, but it was blocked by a virtual "moat" of spiny cactus.

Fargo knew the Ovaro could make the jump, but if his rear hocks bent too much in this loose sand, he'd likely pull up lame. So, instead, Fargo reined his horse in to a canter, then copied a battle trick he'd learned from the Cheyenne: He planted both hands in the saddle, lifted himself, rotated around, and plopped backward into the saddle.

Fargo now stared at his enemy as he snatched his 16-shot Henry rifle from its boot and jacked a round into the chamber. Unable to believe what he was seeing, Crawley stared in slack-jawed idiocy as Fargo's rifle spoke its piece over and over.

Fargo was sitting too awkwardly, and firing at a moving target from another moving target, and he doubted his ability to hit men at this distance. In a run-down to the death, however, Fargo played by his own rules. He dropped a bead on the blood bay's massive chest and levered the breech, spent casing arcing past his face. His next shot made the bay shudder in midair, then crash, rolling, into the pluming dust.

Fargo had no luxury to learn Crawley's fate. Another rider surged forward on a fast coyote dun, a repeating rifle close to finding Fargo's range. Fargo tried to hold the notch dead-center on the stranger's chest as he slowly, evenly took up the trigger slack. The Henry kicked into his shoulder, and Fargo grinned when he saw his shot turn the man hard in his saddle.

These were no Texas Rangers, and Fargo's second tag was enough to send the Committeemen into retreat. But as Fargo watched the pink-and-gold clouds of sunset gather west of Tucson, he realized his hopes rested on a plan so dicey he couldn't even suggest it to himself yet.

"Long story short," Crawley Lake summed up, standing in front of his boss's desk in the lavish library, "Struthers is gut-shot and won't make it. He's in his room right now, howlin' like a moon-crazy coyote. Doc Winslowe doped him, but it keeps bleedin' out through the bullet hole."

Bearcat Lutz had waxed his mustache to lethal points. He rolled one between thumb and forefinger as he watched his lackey from skeptical eyes. "I noticed you limping when you came in. Did Fargo plink you?"

Crawley's breathing increased noticeably and his eyebrows

touched in a frown. "He shot my horse. I got my legs out in time, but I wrenched a knee when I landed."

"I see. You claim you were ambushed, in broad daylight in open desert, by one man. He gut-shoots Struthers, and next rattle out of the box, plugs your horse. Don't blow smoke up my ass, Crawley. *You* ambushed Fargo, my orders be damned."

Crawley's scowling silence was his confession. Favoring his left leg, trailing a reek of whiskey, he flopped into a wing chair and stretched his good leg across a velvet hassock.

"Well, no harm done," Lutz relented, pouring both of them a jolt glass of Scotch. Woo 'em and whip 'em—that, Lutz believed, was the best way to control men, and never let them know which was coming next. "I knew you would disobey me, but I also knew you would fail to kill him. Skye Fargo has harrowed hell itself. My plan is more likely to snare him because it relies on deceit."

"I'll grant he's tough," Crawley said. "Tough as a two-bit steak. But why in the hell *hire* him? No man controls that cock-chafer."

The hallway door yawned inward and both men produced weapons. Lupita stuck her lovely head past the door. "Henry? Will he be back? The tall gringo with the beard?"

Lutz's mouth set itself hard. "What's it to you?"

Her laugh was a silvery, slightly mocking tinkle. "The same thing it would be to any woman who gazed on him. *Un hombre de veras*, a real man."

"See how it is, boss?" Crawley spoke up. "Your own night woman tauntin' you with Fargo. And you want to keep that lanky bastard around?"

Lutz ignored his lackey, eyes like augers boring into Lupita. "Go ahead, you hot-blooded slut, put the horns on me with that saddle tramp. Hachita's had his eye on you for some time."

"Horns? But I am not your wife—unlike her, I know how to please you between the sheets. Your wife will not even let you see her naked. And who would want to see that cow naked?"

Lutz flushed crimson to the roots of his hair. "When Hachita hacks you apart, he'll go slow and start with the little parts."

"Little parts?" she repeated. "Then he should start with you."

Lutz went up like a fuse and reached for the top drawer of his desk.

"Make sure," Lupita spoke up quickly, "that you and the

Hatchet do not kill me before you—*como se dice?*—how you say, 'frame' Reverend Hanchon for rape. I am your only witness."

"Never mind," Lutz snapped, "just get the hell out of here."

"It makes no never mind to me," Crawley remarked after Lupita slammed the door, "but that little Mexer ain't got no match when it comes to all-out bitchery. She must be a savage in the sack, huh?"

Lutz ignored this, studying the other man thoughtfully. "Tell me, Crawley—your accent tells me you're no western native. What did you run from back east? Men only come west to start over."

Startled, Lake's unfinished features eased into a complicit grin. "I had to rabbit—they was a swole-bellied woman in Mississippi waiting on me to marry her."

Lutz nodded. "Ah, yes, you took the old geographic cure. Took it once or twice myself. Anyway, reason I asked—you know how there's huge fortunes being made back in Missouri in outfitting pioneers headed west?"

Crawley paused, leery by nature, before grunting affirmation.

"Why should we cash in at only one end of the western boom? Assuming we can soon control events here in Tucson, I'd like to send you to St. Joe as my agent. You'll have capital to set us up a warehouse. With a small outlay, a man can clear $60,000 a year. That's ten times what most men make in a lifetime. But first we must prevail here."

"We were about to prevail," Crawley reminded him, "and then Fargo drifted into town. Now you've hired him. You can't really trust that do-gooder, can you?"

"No more than I'd trust an Apache to watch my horse. Crawley, you disappoint me. Since nobody in Tucson has the guts to throw down on Fargo, we're going to let the U.S. marshals and God-almighty public opinion back east take care of him for good."

"That's too far north for me, boss. Put it in plain English."

"How plain you need it? By now, any other man harassed the way we've harassed Fargo, since he entered Tucson, would have run like a river when the snow melts. Since I can't kill him, I've hired Fargo to handle the Apache problem. But I didn't tell him *how*, you see. And that's where we're going to kill two nasty birds with one stone."

Fireplace flames reflected in the polish of the floor and furniture, making them glow like ruby embers. For a lazy moment, Bearcat's eyes cut to a go-as-you-please fistfight out on the plaza, two drunk freighters illuminated by a cooking fire.

"The whole city," Lutz resumed, "knows that Fargo is on my payroll. He'll likely try to sabotage me, but his ass is grass because appearances are all I'll need. Have you heard of bichloride of mercury?"

Crawley shook his head.

"I had some freighted in from Yuma. It's used for dressing wounds. But I talked to a contract surgeon from the camp, and it's also a slow-acting poison. If we dump just ten gallons of it into the old Spanish watering hole, the one Eskiminzin's bunch always uses, it'll take twenty-four hours to start killing once they drink it. That means the whole damn tribe will likely die."

"Hell, you've already got plenty of cyanide for leaching ore," Crawley pointed out.

"Too obvious. Cyanide turns the victims' skin blue, and that would point right to the miners. I give Fargo a harmless mixture of water, carbolic acid, and calomel, assuring him it's poison, and tell him to poison the water hole. Of course he won't, but *you* will. We pay a few witnesses to say he dumped the 'poison,' and the federal government has to arrest him for Indian extermination. Congress is filled with spineless Indian lovers."

"Boss," Crawley said, shaking his head in admiration, "that's slicker than cat shit on linoleum."

"I'll grant you this is no job for men who put water behind their whiskey. That red son Eskiminzin has become my hair shirt. I can't even get ore to the smelter at Green Valley. There's plenty of psalm-singers like Hanchon who still hope to see me stretch hemp, but I'll piss on *all* their graves—and that includes Skye God Almighty Fargo."

7

The Trailsman made a cautious return to Tucson under a night sky peppered silver with stars. Bugs swirled around a lantern in the livery barn. Fargo took a careful look into each stall and spotted nothing but a ginger gelding asleep on three legs.

He rubbed the Ovaro down from shoulders to knees, watered him from the stone trough out front, then strapped a nosebag of oats on him and turned him out into the paddock. Fargo washed up quickly at the yard pump, his towel a split flour sack as rough as pumice stone.

"Viejo," Fargo said to the old Mexican as he paid up for another day, "old-timer, is it all right if I spread my blankets in your corral tonight? I'll toss in an extra dollar."

The old man nodded. "But *ten cuidado*, be careful. In Tucson, men who sleep in the open often disappear. Rumor says they appear again two miles north of Tucson—in the clutches of the Hatchet. *Por dios!*"

The hostler made the sign of the cross. His remark caused Fargo a memory stab—Daniel Hanchon's hopelessness, and worse, the old man named Rafe Conlin being whip-sliced up like a side of beef.

"Thanks, I'll be damn careful," Fargo assured him.

He needed to track down Snakeroot, and Fargo suspected he knew where to find him. He walked from Silver Street to the central plaza and left his saddle and rifle at Amy's house. Then he started angling toward the Black Bear saloon.

"Freeze, Fargo, you yellow son of a bitch!"

The hell-for-leather, half-insane tone told Fargo this would be no pissing fight. He turned slowly, gun hand well wide of his holster, to confront a hulking shadow. Tucson had no streetlamps, and very little light spilled from open windows.

"Stranger, what's your dicker with me?" Fargo inquired.

"I'll dicker you right straight into hell, bastard! My name is Josh McKinney. You just up and shot my brother Kinch today with no warning. Turned him into a cripple. Now grab leather, you poltroon!"

Fargo kept his voice calm and deliberate. "Mister, drunk as you are, you wouldn't know a fact from a hole in your head. Your brother pulled down on me. I could have killed him, but I cut him a huss because he was drunk—like you."

"A dirty damn lie. Witnesses told me all about it. Now shuck out that barking iron, Fargo, or I'll smoke you down right now."

The commotion had drawn other shadowy figures, and Fargo feared he'd be back-shot if he didn't play this smart.

"Button your ears back, McKinney, I'm only going to say it once—go home and sober up."

Josh McKinney loosed a string of hot curses. "Just like I figgered it—the big buckskin boy ain't got the stones to face a man fair and square. *Skin* it, Fargo. I double hog-tie dare you to fill your hand, sheep-humper!"

"I tried to reason with you," Fargo said. "Now it's your play."

Fargo went into a slight crouch, eyes never leaving McKinney's hands. McKinney failed to make a clean jerk of his pistol, and Fargo's first slug drilled him dead center in the forehead. The body fell heavily, heels scratching for a few moments, and Fargo instantly went into a deeper crouch and began whirling around in circles with his Colt at the ready.

"Anybody want the balance of these pills?" he demanded.

It worked—this time. The shadowy figures disappeared like ghosts. But Fargo had another reminder of how dangerous it was to remain in town. Yet, for now he had no choice because he rated the Apache menace even more dangerous.

Fargo heard jets of blood slapping onto the stones, but he never troubled himself with the corpse of any man who tried to kill him. Let the "law" deal with it.

As he headed toward the Black Bear, Fargo recalled Crawley Lake and wondered if the strangler survived his hard throw earlier. He veered off toward the Sagebrush Saloon and stood in the shadows, gazing in. No sign of that granite-slab face.

"*Pssst*. Over here, Fargo."

Fargo glanced left, toward Bearcat's almost palatial house, and saw Lupita watching him from an open window. Her smile was restive, as if she harbored secret ideas. He walked over.

"That gunshot just now," she greeted him. "You have killed another cockroach, *verdad*? Who?"

"Nobody I want to brag about. The fool gave me no choice."

"They never will in this town. Come closer, Trailsman."

He did. Candles burning behind her made her dusky skin glow like liquid topaz. Fargo saw she wore nothing but a black lace camisole top, so sheer her chocolate nipples were clearly visible. A mirror on the wall behind her showed Fargo her naked ass, taut but full, high split like a peach. A sudden assault of hot blood stirred his manhood.

"If you are looking for Lutz," she volunteered, "he and that pig's afterbirth Crawley are at a meeting with the—*como se dice*?—how you say, hired guns. Only, they call themselves police."

"So Crawley's alive and well?"

"Not so well. He is limping. I hope you kill them both."

"Those feelings," Fargo said, "don't keep you from sharing Lutz's bed though, huh?"

"So what? Women are not like you men—all we have to do is open our legs and tell each man he is the best. We can do it all night. Bearcat cannot please a woman in bed. Thirty seconds, and he is asleep. But he is very rich and keeps me from the whorehouses. *You*, however, are a woman pleaser. The kind of man we think of while the suet bellies roll on us. I knew it the first time I saw you. Forget Lutz and enjoy these."

One flick of her wrist untied the camisole, and a pair of gorgeous tits were inches away from Fargo's face.

"I don't mind being kissed in dark corners like some wanton," she whispered. "I *am* wanton."

He licked both nipples stiff, and her pulse leaped into her throat. Fargo watched the honey-colored skin throb with her explosive desire.

"Please come inside *now*," she urged him. Her hungry tone squashed any protests.

"That tears it, you little vixen," Fargo said, planting his hands on the windowsill. "Step aside."

He vaulted neatly into the room, landing light as a cat.

"I will make it good for you," she promised. "Look at my thighs, how they shine—you have me hot with desire."

Fargo had bedded some firecrackers before, but Lupita was surely one of the hottest—and most short-fused. This was clearly the master bedroom, and Fargo relished the idea of topping Bearcat's mistress in his own bed. But he was careful to hang his gun belt on a bedpost.

He didn't bother with his boots or shirt, simply dropping his buckskin trousers to his knees. Lupita, her back to him, was hastily clawing a bedcover of intricate crochet work off the sheets. When she turned and saw his hard shaft, leaping high with each heartbeat, she forgot to breathe.

"I knew you would be big like a stallion," she said in a voice turned husky by lust. "No wonder women admire you and men hate you."

She fell back onto the bed and opened her legs wide. "And you will take me like a stallion, *verdad*? In hard, fast, wild plunges that fill me with you."

"Only way I know how," Fargo assured her, centering himself in the saddle and parting the elastic walls of her hot, slick sex as he plunged in deep.

"Ayyy!" she keened, matching him thrust for thrust and digging her nails deep into his muscle-rippling back as he drove her to a screaming ecstasy of repeated climaxes, as if a long string of oiled pearls were being artfully pulled over her own swollen pearl. Fargo held back his explosive release as long as possible, until Lupita was gasping and speaking in rapid, incoherent Spanish. When he finally spent himself, her own final climax shook her entire body.

Both lay, dazed and spent, for uncounted minutes, although Fargo's acute hearing remained on sentry. When the front door of the house thumped shut, he was on his feet in a heartbeat and buckling on his gun belt. Lupita began hastily straightening the bed clothing, which looked like a stampede had gone over it.

"Listen, pretty lady," he said as he headed toward the window. "You're right that Bearcat is low-crawling vermin. All the more reason that you shouldn't help him frame Daniel Hanchon for rape."

"Ya lo veo! Now I understand—you come to my bed hoping to help your *gringa* bitch Amy Hanchon!"

Fargo's jaw went slack with surprise at her peppery retort. He was halfway out the window. "Honey, you called *me* over!"

"*Basta!* Enough!" She placed both hands on his rump and gave a mighty shove. Fargo landed in a heap on the ground, then laughed out loud. Trying to figure out a woman's mind was like trying to prove where all lost years go—so he never tried.

Fargo found the atmosphere inside the Black Bear saloon far less lethal than inside the pro-Bearcat Sagebrush. While patrons did indeed stare at him, the stares were more curious than hostile. The place bristled with weapons, but not one canvas-pantsed, express-gun-toting hard case was in evidence. In Fargo's experience, every boomtown divided into two factions, and this was evidently home to the anti-Bearcat faction.

Cardsharps glanced his way hopefully, but Fargo defeated the temptation to test his pasteboard skills. He had made his point earlier in the Sagebrush, and he didn't favor courting trouble by lingering in public view.

Fargo tried to make out faces in the thick blue pall of tobacco smoke. An old stove with nickel trimmings sat in the middle of the room, and Fargo spotted Snakeroot, so drunk his face was bloated, at the table just beyond it, playing poker with several other men.

The mixed-breed's quarrelsome nature, Fargo quickly realized, had him in hot water again. Fargo drifted close enough to hear better.

". . . sneakin' little half-breed son of a bitch," fumed a man with the pale skin of a miner. "You're peekin' at the deadwood again."

"So what?" Snakeroot retorted. "It's just the discard pile. Those cards ain't in play."

Fargo saw a crimson rage creep into the miner's face. Fargo stepped closer. "Snakeroot, the man is right. You get one warning to stop peeking at the deadwood. If you keep doing it, the first player who complains can claim the entire pot without showing his cards—well within the gambler's code."

"Well, saints and sinners! I've complained three times," the miner exalted, "and now I'm claiming this pot. Thanks, stranger."

"Screw you," Snakeroot protested. "You're just pissed on account you couldn't draw a winning hand all night. I'm pulling my money back out of the pot."

The miner palmed the ivory-gripped Navy Colts he wore on each hip. "I'm about to draw a pair of sixes, 'breed."

Snakeroot looked to Fargo for help.

"I ain't your wet nurse," Fargo told him. "Poker is serious business, and you'd best learn the rules before you get yourself planted."

Snakeroot stared at the pile of silver and gold coins.

"A pair of sixes, huh?" he said to the miner. "That beats none of a kind."

The miner chuckled and began to rake in his winnings. But Snakeroot was too drunk and humiliated to let it go. "*Besa mi culo, maricon*," he muttered as he pushed away from the makeshift table.

"What did you say, greaser?" the miner demanded.

"He said," Fargo cut in quickly," 'Hell, it's only money.'"

"Bullshit," said another player at the table. "I can talk a little Mexer, and that was pure-dee cussin'. I think he called you a queer."

Fargo was getting tired of this barroom bravado. Time was wasting and he had plenty to do. "Boys, let's agree that Snakeroot here is stupidity squared. But you can see he's not heeled, and he's more mouth than he is trouble. Snakeroot, you're out of line. Now apologize."

"Like hell I will! These—*oww*!"

Fargo had grabbed a huge hank of the mixed-breed's long, black hair and tugged it hard. "Apologize, you disrespectful mouthpiece, or I'll yank you bald."

"Ah, let it go, Mr. Fargo," the miner relented. "I never killed a man in my life, and I ain't starting with this soft-brain. The skinny sumbitch is crazy as a pet coon."

Relieved, Fargo started tugging his drunk companion toward the door. "C'mon, snap into it before we get shot to stew meat."

"The whole cockeyed world can kiss my ass!" Snakeroot roared out, stumbling to keep up.

"Son, you're a holy show," Fargo muttered. "Until we get our ducks in a row, you *will* be spending less time with O B Joyful."

They emerged onto the shadowy plaza, Fargo's eyes in constant scanning motion.

"Damn you," Snakeroot groused. "I coulda cut that peckerwood into toothpicks, hadn't been for you."

"The ass waggeth his ears. Forget that he-bear talk and forget that frog-sticker on your leg. Hell, you couldn't break an egg with a hammer. You need a good firearm. I've got just the medicine at Amy's house."

"Amy Hanchon," Snakeroot repeated. "One time she rode straddle through town, gave all the white women a hissy fit."

Fargo grinned in the dark. "Yeah, I'll bet plenty of men were thinking about that, too."

"*'Mano*, I'd sure like a taste of that. She any good?"

"Never mind. You'll never taste it talking like that. I bet you lost every peso I gave you, didn't you, big gambler who peeks at the deadwood?"

"Snakeroot!" a Mexican man called out from a donkey-drawn water cart. "I have been thinking of the things you told me earlier. I warn you again, *amigo*—do not take on Bearcat Lutz and, *por dios*, do not try to make common cause with Apache devils. They will smash your head in with rocks just to take your boots."

Fargo couldn't believe his ears. The donkey clopped on past, and Fargo turned to Snakeroot and twisted his shirt, lifting him off the ground. "You damn little toad. I told you to keep all this dark."

"No need to get on your hind legs. Carlos there is flying our colors. He drinks at the Black Bear, not the Sagebrush."

"I don't care if he drinks at Buckingham Palace, I told you to keep our plans dark. From now on you put a stopper on your gob, or you'll be wearing your ass for a hat."

"I ought not to talk so much," Snakeroot confessed. "But I *had* to get pickled, Fargo. This is called Hangtown, but even with all their practice at lynching, they still muck it up. They slapped a man's horse out from under him today, and his foot caught in the stirrups—ripped his head off his neck."

"That's rough," Fargo agreed, his anger easing a bit as he scanned the plaza. "I'll forgive you for getting drunk this time, but not for blatting our plans around."

"There was this one time, I watched the stranglers hang the same man three times before they killed him—plucky bastard asked for a cigarette each time. Got it, too."

They stopped at the Hanchon residence and Fargo knocked three fast, three slow raps, the prearranged signal. The door was unbolted almost immediately.

"Thank God," Amy greeted Fargo, eyeing Snakeroot with wary curiosity. "Come in, both of you. Did you make it to the mine, Skye?"

Fargo had been dreading this. He nodded. "Saw your father, too, and talked to him."

For a moment Fargo feared she was going to swoon. But the russet-haired beauty bravely recovered. "How is he?"

"I won't sugarcoat it, lady, he can't last much longer. If the work doesn't kill him, the beatings will. This entire Committee for Public Safety has to be brought down, and soon. I did try to help your father. Bearcat wasn't home, so I talked to Lupita. It did no good, but I'll try again."

"Talked to Lupita?" she repeated, full lips parting in a smile. "No handsome man just 'talks' to her."

However, she was too worried about her father to act miffed, Fargo noticed gratefully.

By now they were all seated in the salon. Amy fought valiantly to resist tears.

"Oh, *why* did we come all the way out here? How vividly I remember when father and I stayed at the Patee House in St. Joseph, the finest hotel west of the Mississippi. You could summon a maid just by pulling a velvet rope."

She took a lace-edged handkerchief from her bodice and dabbed at her shining eyes. "I never expected toppers and silk cravats in Tucson, but open murder? Where is the law—*any* law?"

"I wish it could be federal starmen or at least honest soldiers," Fargo replied. "Instead, it'll have to be us. And with luck, a little help from the Apaches."

"The Apaches?" Amy and Snakeroot exclaimed together.

"Like I said, there's no soldiers, no marshals, no honest vigilance group. There's plenty in Tucson would like to see Crawley and Bearcat dance on air, but they're scared. Since Lutz is hell-bent on exterminating the Apaches, I have to make medicine with Eskiminzin."

Fargo looked at Snakeroot. "This is where I need your translating skills. As soon as I talk to Lutz, and find out his exact plan, you and I are riding south to Eskiminzin's camp. Where do you keep your horse?"

Snakeroot flushed. "Ain't got one. Never did. I can't ride."

"Can't . . . ? You said you were a horse peeler."

"I lied. I've got piles," Snakeroot admitted. "So bad I can't ride."

Fargo looked at Amy, and despite the tension they both burst out laughing. "Yeah, Snakeroot, you're a real bravo. Can you at least talk Apache?"

"Hell yeah."

"All right, that's mainly what I need from you. Do the stranglers have a powder magazine?"

The mixed-breed nodded. "The boarded-up dance hall you asked about. The back end of the building."

"All right. When the time seems best, me and you will take care of it. We could use some help with all this, though."

He gazed at Amy, who looked fresh in a sprigged muslin dress. "You mentioned your father's political faction. Will they fight?"

"Many go to his church. They're all hard-working, and many are brave. But none is a soldier, and Lutz has already 'arrested' several of the leaders."

Fargo glanced at Snakeroot as if sizing him up. "I told you back in the Black Bear that I had the medicine you need. Way things are looking, I might's well give it to you."

He went to his saddle, behind the door, and returned with a Remington single-action revolver. "I won this in a poker game in Durango, Mexico. It was ball and cap, but I liked it so much I had it rechambered for factory ammo. You know how to use it?"

Snakeroot took the weapon. "This pin drops the cylinder for loading. This doohickey on the side ejects the spent cartridge when you pull it back. You revolve the cylinder to the next chamber each time you cock the hammer."

Fargo nodded. "Sounds like you *might* be able to hit the inside of a tent. Far as actually shooting it, there's only one rule that matters: Don't squeeze off your round until you know you can't miss. It's not the first shot that matters, it's the first hit."

Snakeroot tucked it into his sash but behind his shirt.

"Leave the hammer on an empty cylinder," Fargo warned, "so you don't shoot your—" he glanced over at Amy—"kneecap off."

Snakeroot stood up. "I better turn in. I sleep in a hogshead on the plaza." He peeked at Amy's cameo-perfect beauty and grinned wickedly. "How 'bout you, Fargo? Got a place to bed down?"

"Would you care to expand on that boorish remark?" Amy demanded.

Snakeroot scuttled toward the door. "Lady, I don't even know what you just asked me. My apologies. *Solo en broma*, eh? Just kidding. *Hasta luego*."

"Don't be flashing that gun around," Fargo ordered, following him to the door and lifting the heavy bar. "You won't need it until later."

"I'm half Mexican, Fargo. I prefer the blade."

"Well how about it?" Amy teased Fargo when they were alone. "You don't have to stay here, but why not come upstairs with me for a while. Maybe tuck me in?"

"Amy, you fetching little siren, if I was ever tempted. But I did a lot of crawling under a hot desert sun today, and things will get even rougher tomorrow. I better get back to the livery and turn in."

All that was true, but Fargo left out the real reason for his exhaustion—his earlier bedroom acrobatics with Lupita. Amy seemed to pluck that thought from his head.

"Well, for you the offer is open. You know, Skye, men like you aren't meant for one woman. No woman would want you for a husband, but, oh, do we *want* you."

Fargo stood up to leave, immodestly smiling at the truth of what she said. But his smile faded when he asked her, "How 'bout you— got a gun?"

"Several, and father taught me how to use them. He told me once that his God was the Old Testament God, not the turn-the-other-cheek kind."

"Good, but from now on have them to hand at all times. A gun is generally no use if it's in a drawer. Anybody forces his way in, give him some of that Old Testament religion."

8

Lugging his saddle, Fargo moved cautiously along the central plaza, grateful for the moon shadows but with his right palm resting on the butt of his Colt. Near saloon row, drunks shot at the moon, and somebody had doused a goat with kerosene and set it ablaze. It ran, bleating, while the drunks took pot shots at it.

"Reg'lar little piece of heaven," Fargo muttered, realizing again how little use he had for settlements. Seemed like everything rotten—smallpox, syphilis, crime, taxes on the meat a man eats—started in settlements. Then again, Fargo admitted, he rarely plucked an Amy or Lupita off a mesquite tree.

Nighttime temperatures in Tucson were often forty degrees cooler than daytime, and Fargo spread his blankets in a corner of the corral near sagebrush to break the force of the wind. He knew the nearby Ovaro would give his trouble whicker if interlopers came, and all the half-wild dogs who slept nearby were another ally.

Thus reassured, Fargo slept the sleep of the just until bird chatter woke him at sunrise. Although he was not a superstitious man, he was greeted by a sight that, for him, had become an omen: the sun coming up while a full moon was setting. Every time he saw it, he ended up in somebody's sights.

"Yessir, I'm mighty damn blessed," Fargo said, watching the lazy vaporing of his breath in the crisp morning air.

He took crumbled-bark kindling from a saddle pocket, built a small cooking fire with gnarled mesquite wood, then mixed corn meal and water into little balls and tossed them in the hot ashes to bake. His hunger slaked, Fargo whistled in the Ovaro and tacked him.

A plan had come to Fargo during the night, one based on his careful scrutiny of the Lady Luck mine yesterday. If anything went wrong, his only hope would be the Ovaro's strong wind and limbs. So Fargo took the time to inspect saddle and pad for burrs, then tested the cinches, latigos, and stirrups. Last he inspected the halter and reins for worn spots.

He forked leather and was just emerging onto the plaza when a voice bellowed, "Fargo!"

In an eyeblink Fargo had lowered himself in the saddle and skinned back his Colt.

"Chrissakes, don't shoot! I got a message from Bearcat."

Fargo spotted the speaker and recognized him as one of the men who came to Amy's house two nights ago.

"You got a stutter?" Fargo demanded. "Spit it out."

"Bearcat needs to see you as soon as possible. He's waiting at his place."

Fargo spurred toward the east side of the plaza, where Lutz's huge lumber home was the centerpiece. As Fargo rode past the boarded-up dance hall, he eyed it carefully for the best entrance. Destroying all the ammunition in the powder magazine wasn't possible without blowing up half the town. But it could be silently "compromised," perhaps weakening any attacks by the stranglers.

Fargo hitched the Ovaro to a tie-rail in front of the library windows so he could watch the stallion—the Ovaro had always been a magnet for horse thieves. An elderly mestiza servant let Fargo in at the front door and led him to the library, where Bearcat Lutz and Crawley Lake waited.

"Morning, Fargo," Lutz greeted him in his take-charge manner. "I'll skip the parsley and get right to the meat. This town is full of saloon gossip. Evidently, that half-breed saloon tout you've been talking chummy with is putting out the story how you and him are going to destroy me. Something about an Apache uprising."

Snakeroot, I'll eat your liver, Fargo fumed while keeping his face bored and amused.

"Snakeroot?" Fargo snorted. "Whoever started that stretcher is grazing loco weed. He's an amusing character, but he's all mouth. He's got piles so bad he can't even set a horse. At the first gunshot he'd show the white feather."

"Hunh. You know, Crawley said exactly the same thing about him. You two agree on some things, at least."

"Speaking of Crawley," Fargo said, "I hear your 'ramrod' here bollixed up a lynching yesterday. He also failed to kill me in an ambush. They say a new broom sweeps clean—why don't I just plug him now and take over his job?"

Crawley's slab face turned livid. "In a pig's ass, you arrogant son of a bitch."

Lutz stroked his silver goatee. "That attack on you, by the way, was Crawley's brainchild, not mine."

"Oh, Crawley signed his own death warrant yesterday," Fargo said calmly, "when he made his piss-poor attempt to kill me. It's past peace-piping now."

Crawley fidgeted nervously, but lost none of his bravado. "That's mighty tall talk, Fargo. You must have a set of oysters on you, huh?"

Fargo gestured toward the thug's holster. "That cutaway holster is just a false front, like the ears pinned to your vest. A back-shooting coward like you shouldn't pretend to be a draw-shoot killer."

"Stow it, Fargo," Crawley growled, "before I—"

"Ease off, Crawley," Lutz cut in. "Fargo, I'm not one to nose a man's back-trail. But every time I hear about you, you're fighting for the law-and-order side."

"Sometimes that side pays best, but most of what you hear is homegrown Robin Hood tripe. The dirt scratchers and perfumed clerks need their folk legends. Jim Bowie invents a knife, and next thing you know he's killed a hundred Mexicans at the Alamo with it. I'm telling you, I ride for the money, not the brand."

"Well, you're mighty convincing, Fargo. No offense, but I hope you will consider the consequences if you try to play it foxy."

"The only consequence I care about," Fargo said, "is the bonus you're paying."

"*That's* the spirit that's proving up the West!"

Lutz snapped his fingers and Crawley, eyes never leaving Fargo, went through a door into an adjoining room.

"Now that we're alone, Fargo, here's something curious. I found Lupita fast asleep last night with bite marks on her tits and smelling of male sweat."

"I never eat off another man's plate," Fargo lied sincerely.

Bearcat, looking unconvinced, nodded anyway. "You seem like a square dealer, but how do I know you're not a four-flusher?"

Fargo twitched a shoulder. "This game could get old," he countered. "How do I know that you ain't playing ring-around-the-rosy with me?"

Lutz laughed in his hearty, phony way.

"You *should* work for me," he urged Fargo. "Sure, you bag plenty of poon in your travels, but, Christ, where is your wealth? For men like us, men of no-church conscience, opportunities abound."

"The silver will play out," Fargo reminded him. "Even up on the Comstock, and there's no lodes like that down here, just isolated veins."

"Hell yes, it will play out. But soon a bovine gold rush is coming to the West."

"Not if war breaks out back east," Fargo said.

"That will just delay the inevitable. Predictions now have a four-dollar longhorn selling for forty dollars at market. Money will flow in this region, and the man at the top will be the king maker in a new land."

"East Texas, maybe," Fargo said. "The grass is too poor out here."

"All right, then, Tucson could become like St. Joe's—a stepping-off place for folks following the Gila Bend route to California. Especially with this new El Paso to Fort Yuma road. I could be running this territory in a year or so, Fargo, and with you siding me, we could run our own fiefdom."

Fargo pretended to mull all this. "Side you how? I'm no businessman or miner."

"Your job would be to clear the profit path of all that encumbers it. I have no gripe with Daniel Hanchon and the other psalm-singers until they block that path."

Crawley returned lugging a ten-gallon milk can.

"Speaking of clearing the path," Lutz said, "those flea-bitten Apaches under Eskiminzin are always on the scrap. I've tried to bribe them with loads of trinkets, but they always kill the freighter who brings them."

Lutz nodded toward the milk can. "No more trinkets. It's time to snuff their wicks for good. Daniel Hanchon preaches how Indians have souls, but Hanchon is a sweet-lavender idiot. Clearing the freight roads, that's the main mile, Fargo. These gut-eating savages haven't even harnessed the damn *wheel*. Except for the civilized Cherokees, none of these tribes even records its own language. Souls? Let's be honest, Fargo, these aren't even human beings."

"Souls ain't in my line," Fargo said casually. "Oh, I won't enjoy killing them, but I won't need a crying towel, neither. It's just a job."

He pointed his chin at the can. "But how do I kill them, drown them in milk?"

Crawley snorted. "That ain't milk, it's a reg'lar tonic for what ails 'em. *If* you got the hard in you to use it, which I doubt."

"Shut your pie hole," Bearcat snapped at his lackey. "It's poison, Fargo, virulent poison. Eskiminzin's bunch have taken over an old Mexican village about fifteen miles southwest of here. They have one source of water, an old Spanish watering hole. Ten gallons of this will wipe them all out."

The words hung in the air like a rotten smell. Fargo looked skeptical. "Apaches aren't cattle—they don't all drink and piss at once."

"That's the beauty of this poison—it takes a full day to kick in. In that desert heat, every one of those featherheads will likely drink before one falls ill. We'll get most if not all."

Fargo didn't care how many Apaches died in a fair fight. But he had all he could do not to draw steel and pop both these slimy sons of bitches over. He trusted neither of these sage rats, and his eyes had kept their hands in sight since he'd arrived.

Crawley Lake took Fargo's delay in answering for hesitation. "Yeah, that Amy Hanchon—now don't *she* fart through silk? Fancy gloves and all, and makin' sure Fargo gets his bell-rope pulled. Be a goddamn shame if a nice little piece like her was to get hurt."

Fargo was in no mood for anything that flowed out of Crawley's filthy sewer.

"You'll be hurting no one, back-shooter," Fargo assured the toady. "Go near her, and I'll feed your guts to your asshole."

Crawley should have wisely let it go. Instead, his right hand inched closer to the walnut butt of his six-gun.

Fargo's face turned into a chiseled warning. "Put some air between your hand and that holster, strangler."

"Kiss my lily-white ass, Fargo. You don't run me."

Even before Crawley's last word was out, Fargo pulled the Arkansas Toothpick from his boot, tossed it with impressive strength, and pinned Crawley's right sleeve tight to the arm of the chair. Gun drawn, Fargo crossed to the chair. He cuffed Lake hard and repeatedly, splitting his lips and sending flecks of blood in all directions.

Fargo jerked his knife free, backed away from the chair, and leathered his Colt. "Stand up and pull steel, you murdering, white-livered pig. *Pull* it. No? Are you mad at me, slab face? Real mad, shootin' mad? Mad enough to kill me? Well, here's your big chance."

Crawley's battered face flamed red. He sat motionless as a statue, his bloody lips quivering and the muscles of his throat twitching.

"You sniveling, cowardly, dry-gulching mange pot," Fargo said in disgust, "I'm serving notice right now—I *will* have your guts for garters. Take a good look at this face, you milk-kneed braggart. I'm the man who will soon send you to eternal flames."

Lutz was both impressed and slightly shaken by Fargo's calm, lethal display. "Well, Fargo, looks like I *did* hire the right man. You're colder than last night's mashed potatoes. Few men can take the vinegar out of Crawley as you just did."

Lake swore, then stomped from the library, slamming the door so hard a picture fell off the wall. Fargo lifted the lid of the milk can and sniffed. From years of riding into plague-stricken towns, he recognized the astringent smell of carbolic acid—a disinfectant, but surely no "virulent" poison. With that one whiff, his hunch was confirmed.

"Ready to take it to their water hole?" Lutz asked.

"It'd be suicide in broad daylight. Besides, I always scout an area first. Just keep that poison hidden good, and I'll be back for it soon."

Fargo did indeed intend to scout the Apache camp, but he had an even more pressing task—to give Daniel Hanchon and the rest of the prisoners at the Lady Luck a splinter of hope while also rattling the confidence of the guards. Yet, it had to be done so that Fargo wasn't linked to it, or Hanchon might pay for it. In fact, it had to pass for a routine hazard in the mining game.

He crossed the Santa Cruz River and bore north toward the foothills and Lutz's silver mine. His study of the terrain yesterday had left the safest possible route imprinted on his mind, a route with minimal ambush points. He approached to within sight of the mine without one sign of Apaches.

This time, however, he did not hobble the Ovaro in the rock declivity and retrace his journey up the front slope. Instead, he rode into an erosion ditch made by flash flooding out of the nearby

Coronado Hills. It wended its way to the steep back slope of the mine.

Fargo hobbled his Ovaro in the erosion ditch and again left his Henry in its saddle scabbard. He knew he had to avoid a shooting scrape. Even Lutz's mudsill ruffians, most of them poor marksmen, were dangerous in numbers. Nor did he want to be recognized.

Thinking all that, Fargo removed the rawhide hobbles and instead threw the reins forward. The Ovaro was trained to stand still when he could see the reins, and this way he might eventually save himself if Fargo didn't make it back.

As he scrabbled his way up the rocky back slope, Fargo kept a worried eye on the ridge behind him. The small prison, protected by its palisade of sharpened stakes, straddled that ridge. An outlying sentry carried a fifteen-pound Sharps, the most accurate buffalo gun of the day. It was common for a Sharps to score hits at eight hundred yards, and Fargo was only about half that distance away.

"Fargo," the Trailsman muttered to himself, "if brains were horse shit, you'd have a clean corral."

He sought out large boulders for cover, moving up the slope in quick spurts except where loose talus or shale forced him to plan each step. He crawled carefully over the lip of the slope and looked down on the busy mining operation.

Fargo spotted Daniel Hanchon immediately, one shoulder pushing a car heaped with ore tailings and looking like a dead man walking. Hachita, up near the assay shack, was busy laying his razored whip across the shoulders of a man who had collapsed to the ground. The look of ecstasy on the evil bastard's face made Fargo think of a man in the throes of bedroom pleasure.

He spotted Hamp Johnson, too, the other mad dog Fargo had seen yesterday, and a grin twitched at Fargo's lips. If Johnson remained where he stood, leisurely enjoying a cigarette, Fargo's dicey plan might bear bloody dividends.

Yesterday, with an eye honed by a life on the frontier, Fargo had especially noticed this steep slope—at least fifty degrees, he guessed—flowing down from his present position directly toward the guard barracks. And the amateurish miners had ignored "angle of repose," or the exact slant where debris will move at the slightest force. In his greed, Lutz had failed to blast out tons of large boulders that were now on the feather edge of a massive rock slide.

Fargo studied the tumbled boulders carefully, more interested in location than in size. He knew his efforts wouldn't be worth a whorehouse token if he picked the wrong boulder. It had to be a linchpin, located so that dislodging it would unleash a chain release. He finally settled on one, and after verifying no prisoners were on this eastern slope, he put his shoulder into it.

Fargo's muscles knotted like thick ropes as he strained. At first it might as well have been the Rock of Gibraltar, but finally he felt it loosen from the ground, then slowly start to roll.

That slow roll became a rapid, violent tumbling as the linchpin quickly set the entire slope into a flowing, dust-billowing wall of death. The guard barracks, and anyone inside, were flattened in seconds. Hamp Johnson, slow to react, loosed an unheard scream before being crushed to paste.

Fargo began his escape, aided by the dust. He took no pleasure in any man's death, but this was frontier war now, no rangers, no marshals, no soldiers, and the odds were against him. They struck first, three days ago on the plaza, and now the hell-spawned vermin would reap the whirlwind.

9

Following a hunch, Fargo found Snakeroot on the central plaza touting for the Black Bear saloon. His mood was sullen and apathetic, the result, Fargo figured, of the pungent mescal he could smell on the mixed-breed's breath.

"If you weren't such a skinny runt," he greeted the tout, "I'd thrash you sick and silly. Thanks to your mouth swinging way too loose, Lutz suspects what we're up to."

"Ah, this hole is fueled by lies and rumors. The Bearcat can't know what's true and what's not."

Fargo grinned. "Glad to hear that. Should help you nerve up for today's mission."

"Mission? *Vaya!* Missions are for priests."

As Fargo explained, Snakeroot's eyes almost popped their sockets.

"Are you loco?" he demanded when Fargo fell silent. "Just ride into Eskiminzin's village, bold as a big man's ass? They'll feed us to their dogs."

"An Indian is a curious creature," Fargo argued. "I'm going to set up a parley pole. That way they'll know I have something to tell them, and they'll want to hear it."

"And *then* they kill us."

"Maybe," Fargo admitted, carefully watching passersby. "Indians are also notional."

"You're telling that to me? My mother was Apache."

"All the more reason why you should go with me. We're trying to help Eskiminzin's people avoid being wiped out."

"*Que lastima,*" Snakeroot said scornfully.

Fargo nodded. "You're right, it *is* a pity. It could drive all the tribes out west into war council, and that could kill every settler in Arizona and New Mexico. That's why I need you to translate."

"Fargo, I told you about my piles. I can't—"

"You'll be using a sheepskin pad for a saddle. And I rented you a mule—easier gait than a horse. C'mon, we're burning daylight."

With Snakeroot still protesting, Fargo grabbed his elbow and tugged him in the direction of the livery.

"Hell of a racket from north of town earlier," Snakeroot said. "Sounded like a rock slide. Dust is still hovering."

"Accidents happen. Hope nobody got hurt."

Snakeroot snorted. "So it *was* you. But listen, Fargo. You ain't stupid enough to believe that me being half Apache will help you, are you? The other half of my blood is Mexican, and Apaches hate Mexicans more than they hate whites."

"Hell, that's old news. Mexicans pay a bounty for Apache scalps."

"That's not all. The beaners not only murder them, they bury them facedown. You know what that means."

Fargo nodded. "That way, Apaches believe, they will never see the Place Beyond the Sun. But never mind all that. You speak Apache, and that's what I need."

"Fargo, I—"

"You know, Snakeroot," Fargo cut him off, "not every drop of rain is meant to get *you* wet. Just nerve up. Stay calm and let me run the show."

"'Nerve up.' Easy for you to say."

At the livery, Fargo noted with approval that Snakeroot at least knew how to tack the mule. He even thought to examine its hooves.

"You got that Remington I loaned you?" Fargo asked as he snugged the girth.

"Tucked behind my shirt. Damn thing keeps poking my pizzle."

"Never mind, just remember—that gun *might* be necessary if Lutz's peckerwoods ambush us. But once we get into Apache country, do not unlimber unless it's life or death. They expect us to wear weapons, but actually drawing them will leave us buzzard bait."

"*Vaya!* You weren't talking that life-or-death manure when you hired me."

Fargo grunted. "The high wages shoulda told you that. Just take all your complaints and bottle them. Keep your mind clear and your eyes to all sides. Now, let's get a wiggle on."

A moment later Snakeroot, after two false starts, managed to swing up and over. Instantly, the mule bucked hard, and Snakeroot was launched like a stone from a catapult. He turned a midair somersault and flew into an empty stall, luckily one lined with straw.

Fargo, still holding the Ovaro's bridle, laughed so hard he had to double up. "You damn fool, you never mount a mule inside a building. Lead him outside."

Cursing like a stable sergeant, Snakeroot led the mule into the yard behind Fargo and his pinto. Fargo took a moment to draw his Colt and palm the wheel, checking the action. Then he loosened the Henry in its boot and looked at Snakeroot.

"All right, Apache warrior. I figure we can reach their village in two hours. Let's get this medicine show on the road."

They bore southeast through shimmering desert heat that dried the moisture from the surfaces of their eyeballs. Looking south toward Mexico, Fargo always saw a line of dark scarps on the horizon, and country so open and vast there was no clear line where near became far.

"This heat will dry us to jerky," Snakeroot fretted.

"This ain't bad," Fargo said. "Once, the army tried to build a short-line railroad between Tumacacori and Nogales, just south of here. Heat warped the train rails."

Unscouted country was the most dangerous, so as the two riders drew nearer to the Apache stronghold, Fargo deviated from the trail to sweep their flanks and climb the high ridges and spines. It didn't take his experienced eyes long to confirm that the two men were being watched.

"Stay frosty," Fargo told Snakeroot, returning from a nearby ridge.

"Trouble?" he demanded.

"Maybe. Maybe not."

"Apaches?"

Fargo shrugged. "Unless they're sunburned Frenchmen."

"Ah, cowplop!" Snakeroot snapped. "Don't you *ever* answer a question on the square?"

"All right," Fargo said. "There's hundreds of red devils getting set to jump us. Most likely, they'll slit us open and feed our hot guts to their dogs while we watch. You prefer *that* answer?"

"Jesus Christ, Fargo." Snakeroot paled. "You serious?"

"No, but the game is going to get rough, so put a stopper on your gob and pay attention around you."

Rocks caked with silt dotted the bottoms and dry washes. A series of sandstone ledges rose above the trail on both sides. Fargo's eyes had been scouring them as he rode.

"Fargo! Fargo, do you—"

"Damnit, Snakeroot, wipe your nose. Don't point like a scared schoolgirl. I see him. Don't stare at him, and don't raise your voice. Just keep riding, hear? Look bored, not scared. That Apache is no more of a surprise to you than a red-tailed hawk."

"Hell, he's got a rifle aimed at us."

"Yeah, a Jennings rifle, to put a fine point on it. And being Apache, he likely knows how to use it. Most tribes think magic guides bullets to the target, but Apaches aim."

Fargo held the Ovaro to a trot, switching hands on the reins to rest his arms. By now they were riding through canyon walls marked with dramatic striation, and more and more Apache braves were showing themselves. It was easy to tell they were forced to raiding and foraging to survive—the only piece of clothing common to all of them was the bright red sweatband that also kept the long, coarse, black hair from their eyes. Otherwise, their clothing ranged from blue cavalry trousers with yellow piping to buckskins like Fargo's.

"*Hijo*," Snakeroot swore behind Fargo. At first the mixed-breed was rendered witless by terror. Then, watching Fargo move stoically forward, Snakeroot forced the terror from his face.

"Hell, they look like statues," he said. "Just watching us."

"They're damn cunning," Fargo said. "I've known them to time a crime so that hard rains wipe out their escape trail."

"A few of them only got stone-tipped spears, but I hear they'll go through you like spit through a trumpet."

Fargo nodded. "No people to fool with."

"Lutz can't figure that out."

"His type will never crater—too ambitious. He'll have to be killed."

The narrow trail topped a small rise, and Fargo spotted a water hole about the size of a large kitchen garden. It was surrounded by gradual slopes covered with stubby jack pine.

"Light down and tether that jenny," Fargo told his companion. "I'm setting up the parley pole."

Fargo unlashed a four-foot-long pine pole from his saddle, borrowed from the wood pile at the livery. One end had been sharpened; to the other, scraps of red-painted rawhide had been tied. Using a spare horseshoe, he pounded it into the ground in plain view of the watchers above.

"This will work?" Snakeroot asked, dubious eyes watching the pole.

"With Apaches it's hard to say," Fargo replied. "I see their contrary nature in you. They trust no one, and why should they? But at least now they know we want to make medicine with them."

"Wait a minute," Snakeroot said. "When whites request a parley, ain't they s'pose to give the Indians a bunch of damn flub dubs—mirrors and combs and such?"

Fargo touched the doeskin bag on his belt. "I might have something even better."

"What?"

But Fargo ignored Snakeroot, watching an imposing figure climb down from the sandstone ledge above them. "Here's the fandango."

"All the saints," Snakeroot muttered. "That's him, ain't it? First time I ever laid eyes on him, and I can tell it's him."

Fargo nodded. "That's Eskiminzin, all right. All grit and a yard wide."

Apache men were muscular in general, especially in the legs and chests, but Eskiminzin's muscles literally stood out from all the rest. It was said he once pulled a running buffalo down, and watching him approach, Fargo could believe it.

Eskiminzin carried an old Cavalry carbine, but did not aim it. He moved in so close that Fargo could see beggar lice leaping from his clothing.

"Que quieres?" he demanded in Spanish. "What do you want?"

Fargo understood and turned to Snakeroot. "Tell him we want to make common cause with Eskiminzin. Tell him the white-eyes in Tucson plan to poison his people."

Fargo assumed, since Snakeroot also spoke Spanish, that he would stick to that language since the Apache used it. Instead, he started out in guttural Apache, tearing a snarl of rage from the battle chief. He brought the carbine's muzzle up to Snakeroot's face and unleashed a string of rapid Spanish, too fast for Fargo.

"He says," Snakeroot reported after swallowing audibly, "that I have no right to speak the People's tongue. I am a whoreson traitor to the People. If I use Apache again, he will cut out my tongue.

Also, he thinks we are spies for Bearcat Lutz and must go before council."

"I meant to hold this back," Fargo said, "but it's time to post the pony."

From his doeskin bag he removed a pale white moonstone painted with blue hailstone designs. He handed it to Eskiminzin, whose hard, deeply seamed face softened in wonder at seeing it.

"The hell's your grift?" Snakeroot demanded in English.

"Never mind," Fargo told him, nervously watching the clan leader's reaction to this new tact. That stone was given to Fargo by the Navajo Chief Cohate after Fargo saved scores of Navajo children from *Comanchero* slavers. The message of that stone was clear to any Southern Plains Indian: *Whoever owns this stone is a true brother of the red man.*

But Navajos and Apaches, though closely related, often warred with each other and even sold each other's children to slavers, and Fargo wasn't sure what Eskiminzin would do. Abruptly, the clan leader's coldly autocratic manner fell away.

"I know you now," he said in Spanish Fargo could mostly follow. "At first I thought you were here to trick us into the prison at Bosque Redondo. But this stone . . . the Navajos call you Son of Light. Any white-skin who would risk his life for red men must be respected. I have ears for your words."

With Snakeroot translating, Fargo explained the lethal treachery afoot. "Eskiminzin, I make war against no people, my own included. But when cowards resort to murder instead of giving their enemy a fighting chance, they become vermin that all honorable men must crush."

"I have ears for such words. Real words I can pick up and put in my parfleche, words with weight."

Realizing that friends had arrived, Eskiminzin's extended clan joined the men on the trail. Only the young children were shy. Their glances touched Fargo or Snakeroot and quickly slid away.

"Lutz and his killers," Fargo continued, "plan to poison your water hole and make it look like I did it. But Lutz knows I wouldn't actually do it, that I'd pour it out in the desert. So the poison he's giving me isn't really poison at all, just something witnesses will see me riding out with."

Eskiminzin nodded. "The real poison will be brought out later that same night, and you will bear the stink of this crime."

"Preciso."

"This is Lutz. When the sun sets in the east," Eskiminzin said, "that is when I will trust the white-eyes."

Unnoticed, a small boy had crept up to Snakeroot while the latter translated. He whipped up Snakeroot's right pants leg to expose the Spanish dag strapped to his leg. The weapon, shaped like a small spade and resembling a child's toy, sent howls of mirth through the Apaches.

"Don't do it," Fargo muttered a warning in English when Snakeroot raised his hand to swat the kid. "Apaches dote on their kids, and they'll kill you if you do it. You ought to know that, you fool."

"Hell, my old lady beat the crap out of me, and she was Apache."

"With that mouth of yours, who could blame her."

Fargo turned to the Apache headman.

"I would not tell Eskiminzin what to do," Fargo said, "but I can suggest a plan I have worked out. If it works, it will help both of us. And perhaps those poor wretches in Lutz's prison."

Snakeroot translated this to Spanish, and Eskiminzin mulled it, his face devoid of emotion. He asked Snakeroot several fast questions, and Fargo listened closely. Fargo's Spanish was limited to the "Spanglish" spoken along the border, but when Eskiminzin switched from the friendly *tu* to the formal *usted*, Fargo stood by for trouble.

"As to the prison," the Apache finally said, "they are mostly white-eyes or Mexicans, and I would gladly kill them with clubs as I would a snake. But if it helps Son of Light to free them, it must be done. As to my people and the poisoned water, speak this plan of yours."

"Katy Christ!" Crawley Lake swore. "You act like this is all just tiddlywinks. Hamp Johnson got squashed so flat he's only got one side."

"Rock slides at mining sites," Bearcat Lutz said patiently, "are common as freckles on a redhead. How do you link it to Fargo?"

"Fargo's *here*, ain't he? That fucker's shifty as a creased buck. And he's bulling Amy Hanchon. You think she ain't using her quim to work on him, help her old man out?"

"You're cutting it pretty thin," Bearcat insisted. "I doubt if Fargo is the type to work for his bedroom privileges."

"Bearcat, are you even on this planet? Our pickets saw Fargo head toward the Apache camp, and he was hauling no poison. Why? Ten to one that bastard is talkin' chummy with Eskiminzin right now."

"Come down off your hind legs, Crawley. Fargo told me about this ride. I believe he's scouting, something his type sets great store by. As for Eskiminzin, unless Fargo is a friend of his, which I seriously doubt, there is no way to approach him—he kills whites and Mexicans on sight, so Fargo can't cook up a fox play with him."

"Killing on sight is a wise policy," Crawley agreed. "Take Daniel Hanchon—his mind ain't gone yet, and his body is somehow hanging on. He needs to have an accident before Fargo springs him. He's a big muckety-muck in the church, and people will believe him."

Lutz stood, hands clasped behind his back, in front of tall, lancet-arched windows in his library, giving him an excellent view of the central plaza.

"One dime-novel myth rides into town," he said, "and suddenly all the men are checking in their balls. Granted, Fargo is all man. But once he gets tagged as an Indian exterminator, his hash is cooked."

Lutz turned to look at his subordinate. "Just use your think piece and mull the efficient beauty of it. We have two major flies in the ointment: Fargo and the Apaches. We bring both birds down with one bullet."

"Maybe. There's also that 'breed who's siding Fargo."

Bearcat laughed. "That worthless beanpole? Hell, he's small potatoes. So is Hanchon."

"Amy Hanchon's potatoes ain't so small. What about her?"

"We'll take her out on the prairie."

Crawley's unfinished face went even blanker. "Huh? We're in desert, not prairie."

"It's an old Plains Indian custom. If a young woman is judged to be a slut, all the men in her clan can take her far out onto the prairie. They strip her naked and every man has a whack at her, and the last buck to top her slits her throat when he's done."

Crawley nodded emphatically. "Our . . . clan would dearly love that plan. But most of them boys got fleas and such, so I'm going first."

"Second," Bearcat corrected him. "I bathe daily."

"Anyhow, you'll regret dealing with Fargo. The cat sits by the gopher hole, and so does he."

A Mexican servant brought Lutz a bowl of water, a shaving mug and brush, a towel and razor. Lutz tested the razor on his cheek, then bent over to strop it on his boot.

"Why do you keep letting Fargo gall you?" Lutz asked, lathering his face. "Hell, a man can't always stand up for his pride or he'd never stop fighting."

"Never mind the cracker-barrel lectures," Crawley said. "I ain't in no whistlin' mood. Neither would you be if you had to poison that water hole. Those Apaches catch me, my skin will be stretched out on a tanning rack. Or have you forgot what they done to those mercenaries I hired?"

"No, but that won't happen again," Lutz said confidently. "I've acquired you a coffee grinder."

Crawley's wild eyebrows met in a frown. "Have you been smoking the Chinee pipe? I don't even drink coffee."

"A 'coffee grinder,' you knucklehead, is slang for Richard Gatling's remarkable new gun. Three-hundred bullets a minute. It's still being tested by the army, but it's already got a reputation as an Injun sweeper. Every major post has one in reserve for when they get final approval. I slipped a supply officer a stack of gold cartwheels, and now one of those Gatling guns is hidden in our powder magazine. I'll show you and a few of the boys how to use it before you leave with the poison. I figure that will be tomorrow."

"A Gatling gun," Crawley repeated, visibly impressed. "I seen one a them once at an Independence Day show. That puppy took down the whole wall of a barn."

"Rest assured, the only man who's going to get skinned," Lutz promised him, "is Skye Fargo."

10

Early the next morning, with pockets of mist still hovering over the desert floor, Fargo and Snakeroot rode due east from Tucson in country Fargo had scouted two days earlier. They picked up a feeder creek of the San Pedro river, then angled off into a small brush canyon, climbing down one of its steep sides.

"Boulders choke the head of the canyon," Fargo said, pointing, "and even with tapaderos it's rough riding in this close, spiny brush. Should be safe from horsebackers, 'specially the lazy townies."

Working quickly, the two men built a crude but sturdy jacal or brush hut. Using a new hemp riata he'd bought in Mexico, Fargo tied it to three jack pines and made a triangular rope corral behind the hut. Then both men rode back to Tucson.

"Watch your ampersand," Fargo warned when they parted on the plaza. "And don't get drunk. We should be riding out before sunset."

He turned the Ovaro over to the liveryman on Silver Street and walked the short distance to Amy's house, aware that shadow eyes were on him.

"Skye!" Amy greeted him anxiously at the door, a pincushion pinned to the bodice of her pink gingham dress. "Any new word on Dad?"

Fargo, mindful that his back made a good target, edged past her to get inside. He shut and bolted the door. "Look, before we get into all that again, I have something else to tell you. Get some clothes and personal things packed and ready—no more than a valise."

"My soul alive! What's happened?"

Fargo set his saddle down and propped the Henry against a wall. "Nothing yet, and maybe you won't have to leave at all. But I'm making the first big play tonight. If it goes all right, you can stay here—so long as you stay armed."

She reached into her left sleeve and produced a two-shot derringer with a folding knife under the blade. "There's also a Colt Navy in the umbrella stand near the door. I can fire both weapons. Skye, what if things *don't* go all right tonight?"

"If I'm recognized by any of Lutz's toadies, our lives will be forfeit and you, me, and Snakeroot will have to light a shuck out of here."

"But . . . to where? There's no safe settlement in this region."

"It's no settlement, and it'll mean rough living for a spell, but I think it's safe. Safer than here. It's a brush hut east of town. I've left hardtack, dried fruit, and parched corn there."

"Isn't that area remote?"

"Remote? It's back of beyond, and that's exactly what we need. Apaches control that country, but I told them who you are, and they'll leave you alone."

"Apaches? This 'big play' for tonight—you're talking about freeing my father, right?"

"It's a start along that trail, yeah."

Her face grew more and more skeptical as Fargo quickly outlined his dicey plan for the water hole.

"Right now there's too many guns pointed at us," Fargo concluded. "If this water hole plan works out, there'll be a lot fewer. Plus, I'll likely have grateful Apaches siding me for the raid on the prison. Hacking at the branches of evil won't clean up Tucson—we have to tear it out by the roots."

"Oh, that's eloquent," she said with petulant sarcasm. "Another gold nugget from the Trailsman. Have you at least had a chance to speak with Lupita again about dropping her charge against my father?"

Fargo felt a twinge of guilt. He hadn't really "talked" to her much at all.

"No," he replied, "but I will. Besides, if we can bring the Bearcat down, all his phony charges go with him, and we won't need Lupita."

Amy's anger and frustration were on the verge of boiling over. Her next words were sweet in tone but disparaging. "So it's help the murdering Apaches first? Since you've apparently gone to the blanket, as they say, will you be taking an Apache squaw, too?"

Fargo smote his head in jest. "Now I'm an Indian lover, huh? Frankly, I'd choose a Crow or a Cheyenne. Both are good-looking tribes."

"An Indian lover, yes! What else am I supposed to think?" she demanded, her voice revealing hurt dignity. "In my view of it, you're worrying about fleas while tigers eat my father alive."

"We've plowed this ground before. I told you, it's all one fight," Fargo assured her. "And you started all this when you flagged me down on the plaza."

"I know it," she admitted. "I'm so worried, I'm mixing up my thoughts."

Fargo's manner softened. "It's not the caliber of Lutz's men that bothers me. Hell, they're mostly mossy-horned cattle. But the numbers make me fret. The Apaches are my best choice."

She sighed. "I understand. After your water hole . . . thing, then comes a raid on the prison?"

"That's the big idea, but it's written on water. And this water-hole 'thing' will need at least two days to play out, so be patient."

Misery seemed to sweep over her in a tumult. "But Father and the others won't even know when their turn is coming."

"No need for a conniption fit, muffin. They'll know. I'm sneaking up to the prison tonight before I head out to the water hole."

She flew into his arms so hard that Fargo had to brace himself. "Oh, Skye, *please* forgive my harsh words. How in heaven's name can I ever repay you?"

"Leave heaven's name out of it," Fargo replied, hands cupping the hard swell of her breasts, "and I've got a suggestion."

Fargo rode to Bearcat's house around noon and was told Lutz was out at his mine. But the servant gave him a message from Lutz explaining that the milk can was out back in the stables. He lifted the lid and sniffed—still carbolic acid, noxious but not toxic.

By now Fargo realized that Lutz was trying to frame him. If federals poked into the massacre, which seemed less likely given the turmoil back east, Lutz would admit he hired the Trailsman to deal with the Apaches, but claim he knew nothing of an extermination plan. By pretending to go along with Bearcat so far, Fargo was teetering on a precipice. If his plan failed, he could officially become one of the West's most notorious blackguards.

He lashed the can tightly to the Ovaro using the same cushioning knots employed by teamsters. Fargo knew, as he rode across the plaza, that scores of witnesses were seeing him with that can. And by being conveniently out of town when Fargo picked it up, Lutz was further removed from any crime.

He found Snakeroot on the plaza, carrying a rifle in a buckskin sheath.

"It's a Volcanic lever-action repeater," Snakeroot greeted him. "Borrowed it from my friend Carlos. This son of a buck holds thirty rounds."

"Small-caliber rounds," Fargo pointed out. "And anyhow, I doubt you could hit a bull in the butt with a banjo. But it'll make plenty of noise and sound like several shooters, so bring it along."

Fargo took a quick look at his unlikely ally. "Those rope sandals will be quiet, but leave that Sonora hat at the stables. The straw will reflect light. You won't need a conk cover."

He reached out a hand and pulled Snakeroot up behind him. "Let's go get your jenny."

"Hijo! I'd rather ride a three-legged burro. Ain't it still too early to ride out to the water hole?"

"We got another stop first. You're going to wait with the mounts while I climb up to the prison."

"Por dios! Fargo, they'll shoot you to dog meat. And if Hachita gets you first, he'll slice you up like a side of beef."

"Not unless I stand still and let him. Who'd be that stupid?"

"Fargo, you—"

"Pipe down, you jay. I ain't holding a gun to your head. You told me you'd do anything to stop Bearcat Lutz, and that's what I aim to do. You can stick or quit—make up your mind now."

"Stick," Snakeroot said without hesitation.

"Stout lad," Fargo said in a cheerful voice. "Now let's see can we get you killed."

With the local Apaches now temporary allies, the two riders made better time to the rock declivity where Fargo had left his stallion, two days earlier, within sight of the silver mine.

Even so, after a blazing copper sunset, Fargo had a new worry. Most places in the West this time of year, mosquitoes plagued men and horses all night, flies all day. But the Arizona deserts were too dry for most flying insects, and at night rattlesnakes were the main concern. Numerous after dark, they could badly spook a horse, and a thrown rider could be swarmed by dozens of them before he got to his feet.

"The hell you doing?" Snakeroot demanded when Fargo reined in and dismounted.

"No sense making my horse carry this extra weight," Fargo replied, unlashing the milk can. He poured the contents out into the sand.

"So why you tying the empty can back on?"

"If things go right, I'll need it," Fargo replied. "Never mind all the damn questions and keep your ears and eyes open. I know you grew up in towns, but you're also half Apache. This is where you'll wait for me."

Snakeroot stared toward the dark mass of the rocky plateau behind the mine. A few lights glowed from the prison like distant fireflies.

"You're the boss, Trailsman," he said. "But outside of Tucson, the Bearcat's biggest concentration of killers is right here. I think it's suicide to go up there."

"It'll likely be no Sunday picnic," Fargo agreed. "But why plan on dying? These stranglers ain't up to fighting fettle, and come nighttime they're usually drunk."

Fargo untied his blanket from the cantle straps and wrapped it tightly around his head. Twenty minutes or so later he unwrapped it, and the total darkness had improved his night vision dramatically. He moved out quickly across the moonlit desert, listening for the warning buzz of rattlers.

He made it to the hill where Lady Luck was located and slipped behind it, starting up the steep ridge with its uncertain footing. Even with his improved vision, twice Fargo slid backward on loose shale, hoping it didn't start a slide. Eventually, though, he made it to the top and the encircling palisade of wooden stakes.

This siege fortification was designed to slow down a massed charge, not a single intruder. Fargo wriggled to the inside and flattened himself on the ground, thinking he'd heard gravel scuffed under a boot. He slid the Colt from its holster and waited, thumb on the hammer, listening.

Nothing but the sound of wind-scuttled gravel. Fargo started to push up from the ground when, only yards away, a match flared to life. Hair on his nape rising, Fargo watched Hachita light a skinny black cigar. His face looked like yellowed ivory in the light, the eyes like obsidian buttons, black and hard.

"Fargo!" he bellowed into the dark maw of night. "Fargo, your mother was a whore! Are you out there, *hijo de puta*? Hachita knows who made the rocks slide. I will salt your tail, Trailsman, and then your skull will be my next doorstop!"

Fargo resisted the temptation to kill him now and be done with it. The knife would be silent, but only if Fargo gave the man no chance to fight back, and rarely did the Trailsman kill that way. The last thing he wanted right now was a cartridge session.

So he waited until Hachita moved on, then scrambled toward the low, rectangular prison. Keeping to dark shadows, he pressed one ear to a wall and heard low voices. It was quick work, using the Arkansas Toothpick, to gouge out the mud chinking between two bricks.

"Heads up in there!" he called through the opening. "Is Reverend Hanchon among you?"

A startled silence followed these words. A few moments later, a familiar voice spoke up. "Is that you, Fargo?"

"It's me, Rev. Listen, the rock slide yesterday—did any prisoners catch hell for it?"

"No more hell than usual. So it *was* you? Praise the Lord! Hachita swore it was you, but other guards insisted it was a natural slide. God forgive me, but I rejoiced when Hamp Johnson was crushed to death."

Fargo studied the darkness, recalling how silently Hachita moved. "Any of you prisoners hurt?"

"Ray Nearhood got a small gash, was all."

"Wish I could visit longer, Rev, but I'm up to my neck in two-legged pit vipers out here. I need to tell all you boys to be ready for a hot bust out. I can't say exactly when, but soon—two or three days."

"God be praised. This time, Brother Fargo, I'm taking your advice. Before I beg God to save me, I'll stand up on my own two feet like a man. All of us here will."

"That's the gait," Fargo praised.

Before he could turn away, however, Hanchon's voice arrested him. "There's a line from my seminary Latin, Fargo. It's haunting me now. *Facilis descensus Averno,* 'The road to evil is easy.'"

Fargo felt his heart sink like a stone. Here he was thinking Daniel Hanchon had rallied, and now the old boy was waxing philosophical—not the proper mind-set to survive a bust out under fire.

"Look, that's true, Reverend, but save it for a good sermon. You just keep your eye to the main chance, and when it comes, seize it."

Fargo knew that Bearcat sometimes hired Apache turncoats to watch and report on Eskiminzin's Apaches, and he knew they must be watching now as he and Snakeroot descended the green slopes around the water hole. A quarter moon and patchy stars gave scant light, but deserts were more luminous and the riders visible.

Fearing ambush at every moment, Fargo unlashed the empty can and pretended to pour its contents into the water. The deception, he was confident, wouldn't be detected by distant eyes in this dim light.

"Now see, this I don't get," Snakeroot said.

"The first part of this plan," Fargo explained, "calls for me to earn my pay. I'm *hoping* we're being watched. Lutz gave me no poison, but by taking the risk to come out here to dump the fake stuff, it *looks* like I acted in good faith. Bearcat might be thrown off-kilter."

"So it buys us some time," Snakeroot finished for him. "Keeps him off us long enough to finish the water hole play and hit the prison."

"You're ahead of the roundup," Fargo cautioned. "Don't forget, if I've guessed right, the real poisoning should come later tonight, and I made sure Eskiminzin's bunch won't be in the fight— otherwise Lutz will suspect they know about the plot from me. That means me and you are going to be locking horns with stranglers."

11

Fargo and Snakeroot headed north to Tucson, then swung wide of the trail and doubled back through saguaros, seeking low-lying ground to keep their skyline below the horizon. About a quarter mile from the water hole they hobbled their mounts behind a sandy ridge and completed the trip on foot.

"Fargo, where you from?" Snakeroot asked.

"Why's it matter? We engaged?"

"Friend, you're a stumper. You like to ask questions, but you're not much for answering them."

"Bottle all that park-bench stuff and pay attention to the here and now," Fargo said. "See that barrel cactus west of the water hole? It's good cover for a skinny runt like you. I'll wait behind the stand of prickly pear on the east. I'd say Crawley and his clump of maggots will show up in an hour or two."

"What if they *all* come out?" Snakeroot fretted. "I can't shoot like you do."

"With luck, there won't be much shooting tonight," Fargo said. "With *lots* of luck. I don't think Crawley will bring too many men. That would rouse the Apaches to attack, and besides, if a large posse of stranglers is spotted coming in this direction, it won't help Lutz's frame-up of me."

"Yeah, but I still don't get it," Snakeroot said. "That skunk-bitten coyote won't come by himself. Which means, since we gotta stop them from poisoning the water, that witnesses besides Crawley have got to see you."

"They won't see me," Fargo said, dipping the can in the water hole to fill it, "and Crawley *is* going to poison that water, far as the rest are concerned."

"*Hijo!* I'm sorry I asked. You just say the word, and I'll start blasting away. I've got the Volcanic and that Remington you gave me."

"*Loaned* you."

"Piker," Snakeroot grumbled, disappearing behind the barrel cactus.

Fargo, too, took cover and dragged the sloshing milk can out of sight. This plan had been scratched out in the dirt, and Fargo didn't like the way it hinged on elements he couldn't control. If, for instance, Crawley's men accompanied him too close to the water, Fargo's entire scheme would come a cropper.

Time ticked by slowly, the silence of the desert night almost complete. At times the wind whipped itself into a directionless frenzy, and Fargo was forced to lower his head to avoid stinging grit. Once, a rattlesnake glided right over his boot and Fargo froze, letting it move on.

"There," Fargo finally called over to Snakeroot, "I hear them coming."

But something about the faint noises, approaching from Tucson, bothered Fargo. The tattoo drumbeat of several horses was to be expected, but soon he also detected the jangle of a harness and the hard jouncing of a buckboard. Who would be fool enough to drive a buckboard through Apache country, and why?

"Might be that six-pounder from the town square," Snakeroot offered in explanation. "It's covered with bird shit, but it still works."

"That's a stretch. A cannon's too much trouble to move, and it's worthless against Apaches, if that's who it's for."

There was enough light to make out the dark shape of riders and a conveyance, moving slowly down the slope toward the still pool of water. Fargo counted four riders, a driver, and whoever might be hiding in the conveyance. As Fargo had hoped, all but one remained back—a hulking figure lugging a milk can. Fargo waited until he came abreast of his position.

"How's 'bout I make *you* drink some of that, Crawley?" Fargo said in a low voice.

Lake went as still and silent as a stone lion.

"'S'matter, nun killer," Fargo roweled him hard. "Cat got your tongue? You had plenty to say when you were insulting me and Amy Hanchon and threatening our lives. There's no law out here, and when a man threatens my life, I take him at his word and kill him first."

"Fargo, you're the last man who would murder in cold blood."

"You're right about that."

"Good! Believe me, whatever you're up to here, I'll cooperate."

"You can start," Fargo warned him, steel in his tone, "by moving your gun hand away from that holster. I've already got you notched, and there's no more trigger slack. Just set your can down and take this one. That's it, now keep on moving toward the water."

"Fargo, you don't understand. Bearcat duped you, this ain't poison—"

"I know all that," Fargo said. "Now do what I told you."

"All right. But one word from me, Fargo, and you're a smile in some whore's memories."

"I leave them all smiling, so you'll have to be more specific. Far as your pals up there in the dark, my slug will find a target before theirs does."

"Damn it," Crawley urged, "forget these raggedy-assed redskins and throw in with us, Fargo. Otherwise, for you, it's the knot for sure."

"The big gun-thrower," Fargo said with contempt. "Down to the water, I said, or I'll bullet-snap your spine right now. When you get there, wade in and empty the can."

"All right, it's done," Crawley reported a minute later. "What now?"

"Now," Fargo said, still staying out of sight from the others above, "call up to your men. Say, 'It's done, boys.'"

"The hell for? What are you—?"

The metallic *snick*, when Fargo cocked his short iron, made Lake fall silent. A moment later he did as ordered.

Now, Fargo reflected, with a little more luck Bearcat would believe the water hole was poisoned.

"Hell's waitin' on you, Crawley," Fargo said, leathering his Colt. "Let's open the ball."

"Fargo, you gave your word you wouldn't kill me if I played along."

"Dead wrong, in a manner of speaking. I said I wouldn't *murder* you. A fair fight ain't murder. I also told you it's past peace-piping between us. Twice you tried to murder me, and that's two times too many. Now fill your hand."

Crawley seemed to shrivel up in the scant light, his voice finally registering a tone—abject terror.

"Fargo," he wheedled, "a man's mouth-word is as binding as a writ contract. I promise I'll light out now and never come back. I'll just hit the breeze."

"You'll light out, all right, because you're a white-livered coward. But what about the innocent men you'll murder someplace else, the women you'll rape, the orphans you'll make. No—this is Judgment Day for you."

"Crawley!" an impatient voice called from the group above them. "You draining your snake? Hurry up!"

Fargo knew there was risk in bracing Crawley right here. But he also knew this was Apache country, and those vigilantes were no Indian fighters. At Fargo's first shot, Snakeroot would fire, too, and Fargo was convinced these dough bellies up above on the slope would flee. They would report that Indians drove them out, but not before Crawley poisoned the water.

"I'll shout for help!" Crawley warned. "Damn my eyes if I won't!"

"That just guarantees you'll die. Fight like a man, you've got a chance. I knew I was going to kill you, Crawley, when I saw those ears pinned to your shirt. I can't stomach a back-shooting bully who brags about his murders. Now pull it back—and I guarantee you won't be 'jerked to Jesus.' "

Crawley suddenly turned his back on Fargo. "The Trailsman won't shoot a man in the back."

"No, but a shot to the hip will spin you back aroun—"

Crawley made his move, whirling around with his six-gun spitting orange spears. Caught off guard, with slugs snapping past his ears only inches away, Fargo stuck to his life-or-death rule: Don't shoot until you're sure you'll hit.

Crawley was still wildly blazing away when Fargo's first slug ripped open his heart.

Snakeroot had already opened up with zeal at the group up the slope, levering and firing in a steady stream. Fargo saw one of his random shots strike a vigilante in the eye, and he began bawling like a bay steer. One of the strangler's own men shot him in the head to shut him up. As Fargo had expected from this low bunch, a panicked rider—fearful of Indian attack—peeled away and took off like a house afire. But that left one horseman and the buckboard driver, and why were they neither fleeing nor fighting back?

"Shit," Fargo swore under his breath, "Fargo, you played it too cute."

The blasts from Snakeroot's Volcanic were suddenly and violently drowned out when a Gatling gun opened up like a fiend possessed, attacking the slope below with its deadly hail. Fargo made love to the ground, hearing the cactus all around him being shredded and pulped.

Fargo had scouted for the U.S. Army during testing of the Gatling, and he knew it was difficult to elevate and traverse even for a trained gunner. This one was clearly a novice. With no option but to attack the strong point, Fargo burst from cover and ran a fast, zig-zagging pattern, Colt at the ready.

"Fargo! You double-dealing son of a bitch!"

The lone rider had sheltered behind the buckboard on foot, and now discharged both barrels of his scattergun. Sawing off the barrels reduced accuracy, and the brunt of the buckshot missed Fargo. Several pieces of the lead shot, however, ripped into him like fiery fangs.

With blood streaming into his eyes, Fargo's first and second shots missed, his third blew off the strangler's lower jaw, the fourth tagged his brain. Fargo had one shot left, but when he aimed at the gunner, the last bullet hung fire in the breech, as factory ammo too often did.

It was a race that Fargo won. As the gunner wrestled the cumbersome Gatling around, Fargo jerked the Arkansas Toothpick from his boot and hurled it in a fast overhand snap. A sound like a hammer hitting a melon was followed by a surprised grunt when the big knife punched into the gunner's chest.

"All clear, Snakeroot, if you're still alive," Fargo called out, wiping his blade on the dead gunner's trousers.

"All the saints! Fargo, what *was* that?"

"One giant pain in the ass," Fargo replied, realizing life had just become more complicated. "Just a giant pain in the ass."

Even before Fargo and Snakeroot could retrieve their mounts, at least a dozen Apache warriors, Eskiminzin leading them, appeared out of the darkness like wraiths.

"We heard the fast-talking gun," Eskiminzin explained through

Snakeroot. He looked around at the dead men and grinned. "It did not talk fast enough."

Before Fargo could even parley about it with Eskiminzin, the Apaches began methodically looting and ritually mutilating the bodies.

"Whatever it is, now the gun's ours," Snakeroot gloated. "We'll blast that prison to blow dust."

"Like hell we will," Fargo gainsaid. "A weapon like that is European nonsense. It has to be transported and hidden, and it's almost useless against moving targets. Takes at least two men to work it, both trained."

"Well, at least we can bust it up."

Fargo shook his head. "Nix on that. We're going to make sure Bearcat gets that gun back."

"Fargo, have you joined the peyote soldiers?"

"This is the way of it. Tonight was only part one of the water hole plan. The second part comes tomorrow or the next day when the stranglers will return in force to see if their plan worked. I mean to be with them, so I have to stay in good with Bearcat a little bit longer."

"So what does all that have to do with the gun?"

"Plenty. If that gun is missing, Lutz will know Apaches didn't take it—mechanical devices don't interest them, nor would they herniate themselves hauling it on foot."

"I take your drift," Snakeroot said. "He'll think we have it, and they won't come out here. Plus, we'll be on his shit list for sure."

"The way you say. We need to drive that buckboard back to the outskirts of town, too, dead bodies and all. Everybody knows that Apaches strike there, so we make it look like an Apache raid near town, not trouble out here."

Fargo tipped his head toward the buckboard, where an Apache brave was busy cutting the eyes out of the gunner. "It'll sure's hell *look* like an Apache raid. Those boys don't generally scalp, but they know how to leave their mark."

"Do we take Crawley's body, too? Don't forget that rider who took off when you two gunned it out."

"He couldn't see all that well, and he can't know what happened to Crawley. All the other witnesses, besides us, are either dead or too far away to see much. We'll ask Eskiminzin to carve him up and pump a few arrows in him."

"How'd I do tonight?" Snakeroot asked. "I used up all my ammo and burnt my cheek on the rifle muzzle."

"You're a credit to your dam. You kept it hot enough for me to close in. But let's count our coups later. The night's still young."

Snakeroot and Fargo dragged Crawley's heavy corpse up the slope, where an Apache drove two arrows into it and effortlessly castrated it, cramming the sex organs into Crawley's mouth—an operation neither white man could watch. Fargo and Snakeroot trotted back to their mounts and returned to the corpse-laden buckboard, tying their horses to the tailgate.

"This is just starting, isn't it?" Snakeroot asked as he climbed up onto the board seat.

"'Fraid so," Fargo replied, kicking off the brake. "You're in your first by-god scrape now."

"Yeah, but will it be my last?"

A shake of the reins and the buckboard lurched into motion. "Look on the lighter side," Fargo replied. "They can only kill you once."

"What about that hombre the stranglers hanged three times?"

Fargo said, "Three times—there's a bright side to that, too."

"What?"

"The fellow was well hung."

12

Both men kept their weapons to hand and searched the desert night for attackers as the old buckboard, carrying its grisly cargo, rattled its way north toward Tucson. The horses were nearly played out from hauling the heavy gun to the water hole, and Fargo went easy on them.

"A wagonload of carrion bait," Snakeroot said. "*Hijo!* Think Lutz might get snow in his boots?"

"The world will grow honest first. Look, we're up against it now. It's time to use your ears and eyes, not your mouth."

"All right, I'll pipe down, but I'm saying again you're a fool if you let Lutz's hyenas get that gun back. At least we can destroy it."

"You got it bass-ackwards. Our lives depend on Lutz thinking it *might* have been Apaches that jumped his men. Apaches hit fast and retreat fast, especially near a town. Whatever they don't want they leave alone. Besides, we might not be done with that gun yet, so don't worry about it."

Fargo stood up, knees braced against the dashboard, and stared toward a thin halo of light that was Tucson.

"Can't see any riders skylined, and my stallion ain't giving his trouble whicker. We'll ease in a little closer, then stage our raid. Jump out and check my left saddle pocket. You'll find loads for the Remington."

"How 'bout the Volcanic?"

Fargo snorted. "Hell, you think I run an armory? Never mind it. You'll empty out the Remington and my Colt, I'll empty the Henry's magazine. That's almost thirty shots—that'll pass for a raid. Can you shriek?"

"What, like a woman seeing a mouse?"

"No, you clodpole, like a man with a chipped-flint arrow point in his liver."

"I'll try," Snakeroot promised.

In the saguaro desert just past the fertile cultivation belt, Fargo reined in. The faint tinkle of a piano drifted to their ears, along with shouts and snatches of drunken laughter.

"I figure nobody's likely to check on this until sunrise," Fargo said as they unhitched their mounts and led them well clear. "Not with Apaches in the mix. But we don't want to be seen riding in together. When we're finished, you ride into town from the north, I'll hang back and slip in from the south. Let's hobble our mounts here so the gunfire can't scatter them."

When the stallion and mule were secured, Fargo handed his Colt to Snakeroot. "Don't just blast away fast as you can—scatter your shots in bursts of two and three. It's an ambush."

Fargo slid the Henry from its boot, worked the lever, and said, "Open fire!"

The calm peace of the desert night was abruptly shattered. Fargo emptied his magazine in sporadic shots while the two short irons worked as counterpoint, creating a good impression of a fierce, hectic assault. Snakeroot tried to "shriek," a cross between a coyote howling and a drunk Ute.

"Knock that caterwauling off before they think we're mating," Fargo pleaded, reclaiming his Colt, thumbing reloads into it, and vaulting into the saddle. "I'll look you up tomorrow. Got money for a meal?"

"Yeah. Think we pulled this off, Fargo?"

The Trailsman took up the reins. "Yes and no. Yes, because I don't think Bearcat can prove we killed his men. No, because he's going to be even more suspicious of me than before. Keep that gun hidden, but keep it close."

Fargo quickly rubbed down the stallion and dried him off with an old feed sack. Then he snugged a nose bag filled with oats on the Ovaro and turned him out into the paddock before making the short walk to Amy's house. This quiet corner of Tucson was usually deserted after dark, but Fargo carried his Colt at the ready anyway. If there had been one careless mistake during tonight's double deception, would-be assassins could be lurking anywhere.

Fargo reached Amy's door and gave the prearranged knock quietly—he knew how easily women could be ruined in frontier towns. Once the talk began, "decent" women would draw aside their skirts when the sinner passed, to avoid contamination.

"Skye! Thank God you're alive!" Amy greeted him, quickly drawing him inside and closing the door. Fargo dropped the iron bar into its wall brackets, appreciative eyes taking Amy's measure.

"There was a terrible battle outside of town just now," she fretted. "I'll bet you were in the thick of it."

"Lady, somebody needs to paint you. You look pretty as four aces."

The woman amazed Fargo with her refusal to give up looking feminine and elegant even in this crude, criminal hellhole. She wore a gown of taffeta lace with white satin slippers and gloves.

"Thank you, Skye, but quit stalling. It's we women who can chatter for hours and say nothing. You'll never pull it off."

"Tell you what, let's dicker. If you can scare up a little grub for me, I'll tell you what happened."

"Deal. Help yourself to pulque while I fix it."

Fargo took the decanter from a wall cabinet and crossed to the front-window curtains, peeking carefully onto the central plaza as he sipped the strong cactus liquor. The racket from saloon row seemed quieter—by now, no doubt, the stranglers knew Crawley and the rest were missing. But what else did they believe?

"No silent brooding," Amy's voice admonished him as she returned with his plate. "Come over here and eat while you fill me in."

Fargo did, tying into beans and tortillas while summing up what happened at the water hole and outside of town.

"Will Lutz believe that water was poisoned?" Amy wondered.

"Way I see it, he can't know. But he's got no solid reason to assume it's not. He'll have to check, and that's why I need to be there when he does, like I promised Eskiminzin."

"Skye, Lutz is smarter than his choice of acquaintances might suggest. His miner's court is just like a rustler jury, only it's murder and claim jumping they ignore instead of cow theft. And it's very effective. Don't drop your guard around him."

Fargo nodded. "I've got a god-fear Bearcat is smarter than I credit him."

He rose and looked out the window again. "So far, the signs are good that Bearcat knows nothing yet except there was gunplay, perhaps involving Crawley and an Apache. But you can bet he wonders where I am."

"Care for an alibi?" she teased him.

"I might at that. Curtains are closed—I dare you to strip naked right where you stand."

"I will if you will."

"Square deal," he agreed, unfastening his heavy leather gun belt and dropping it on a chair. In a few shakes he stood naked. It took her longer to strip through more layers, but soon her pendant breasts and beautiful russet mons bush held his gaze riveted.

"Skye, you're ready *now*," she marveled, watching his curved saber leap. "So am I, but there's no place to lie—"

"We'll sit," Fargo said, lowering into one of the sturdy chairs. "You straddling me. I think you'll like it."

"The woman on top?" she said doubtfully. "Can that work?"

She said this last as she was straddling Fargo's lap. He took each minty nipple into his mouth and sucked it, sometimes giving her sharp little pleasure bites that made her beg for more. Fargo bent his staff to the perfect angle, finding the warm, soft portal and pushing just the swollen tip in.

"Don't *tease*," she admonished, wiggling her hips to plunge down his entire length.

The girl who had just been skeptical about "the girl on top" now proved with a vengeance how wrong she was. A woman possessed of indescribable pleasure, she thrashed up and down on him, tits wildly mashing his face.

"Skye!" she gasped, exploding in a delirious chain reaction of climaxes, "different parts of you rub different parts of me! Oh . . . *oh*!"

At least several more times Fargo led her to the erotic peak before her greedy plunges finally broke down his will. His concluding thrashes drove her to one last, bucking frenzy on top him.

"A *mighty* potent force," he muttered when he finally found his voice again.

"Why not stay the rest of the night?" Amy suggested after he'd dressed and she put her chemise back on. "That way we can wake up to more."

"I'm sure that would beat a hot breakfast, but right now I'm not the best man for you to be sleeping near. Not the way these yahoos shoot. Besides, in dangerous times I feel safer outside of buildings. You just be ready, at any moment I come for you, to escape to our hideout."

He hoisted his saddle.

"You'll free Father soon?" she implored.

"Your father soon," he promised in a confident tone, but nagging doubts assailed him.

Fargo was on the plaza just after sunup, sticking to the shadowy margins where snipers couldn't drop a bead on him. As he rounded the front right corner of Lutz's house, a window was thrown up. Fargo tucked, rolled fast, and came up onto his knees with his Colt filling his hand.

"*Ay, Dios!* Do not shoot me, bearded stallion!"

Lupita, her black hair a tangled mane from sleep, hung her upper body out of the window. A black lace bed jacket shamelessly flaunted her caramel breasts and chocolate nipples.

"Do you like danger when you make love, Fargo? Are you man enough to take me with Bearcat pacing in his library?"

"Not with the noise you make, hellcat. I'd be a fool, not a man."

"Yes, it is probably a bad idea," she agreed. "With most men I am quiet, but with a few I am very loud. Never so loud as with you."

"You say Bearcat is pacing in the library?"

"Yes, but Hachita is in there with him. Crawley, whom I call Flat Face, is dead. So are others. They were just now found outside town."

"Does Bearcat blame that on me?"

She gave him a coy, up-and-under pout. "Should he?"

"Of course not," Fargo lied. "We're on the same team."

"You, Fargo, are on your own team. I pray you killed that devil Flat Face—it is one less man in this town to rape me. But Hachita, he is to Crawley as a bull to a calf. They say no man born of woman can kill him."

"*They* are full of sheep-dip, cupcake. The man's insane, that's all. He's dangerous, all right, but men who ought to be killed usually are."

"*Ya lo se.* Even Bearcat, whose own mind is twisted by greed, fears Hachita's madness. But Hachita balks at no order, and for a money hoarder such as Bearcat, he is useful. *Ten cuidado.*"

"I'll be careful, all right," Fargo assured her, going around to the front door.

The mestiza maid led him back to the library, where Bearcat

was indeed pacing. Hachita, bone-handled hatchet and all, sat in a wing chair, cleaning a Sharps Fifty rifle.

"Fargo," Bearcat said when his visitor walked in, "I wondered if I'd ever see you again."

Fargo twitched his shoulders. "Why not? You told me to stop by and tell you how the poisoning went."

Fargo watched the other two men exchange a quick glance.

"Where were you last night?" Bearcat demanded. "After you went to the water hole, I mean?"

"Hold your horses," Fargo said. "Is this about that fandango last night outside of town?"

"Where were you?" Bearcat repeated.

"Well, I'll admit I haven't got a bulletproof alibi. I was with Amy Hanchon."

"With? Or on?"

Fargo waved that off and propped on one corner of Lutz's huge desk. This gave him a clear line of sight to both men. Hachita's blacksnake whip lay coiled under his chair.

Lutz stopped pacing and stared at Fargo. "You're a good liar, aren't you?"

"Middle range," Fargo said modestly.

"There it is again, the drifter humor. Fargo, you won't always be a young man. Men like you get too old for the trail and end up slinging hash for railroad crews."

"What do you care what happens to me? We ain't back-scratching cousins."

Fargo grew alert when Hachita, who was studiously ignoring him, stopped cleaning the Sharps and placed a primer cap on the nipple.

"Ah, cut me some slack," Lutz said, pacing even faster. "I'm just jumpy and suspicious, is all. You see, after I sent you with the poison, I checked my calculations and realized I needed twice the poison you had. So Crawley came out behind you with more."

This was a bald-faced lie, so Fargo answered it with another. "I never spotted him, but then, I kept leaving the trail to avoid ambush."

Bearcat swore. "Why can't Arizona have Indians of the New Mexico type? Shy, moonfaced, take to the Catholic saints and bathing. We get the true savages out here."

Fargo looked at Hachita's burning, barbaric eyes and had to

agree with Lutz. Just then, making the action casual, Hachita thumbed a shell into the breech of the Big Fifty. The moment the long barrel began to swing his way, Fargo's Colt leaped into his fist.

Hachita laughed. "Nervous?"

"Just wise. Clear the breech or ground that weapon."

Hachita refused either option, training his mad, taunting gaze on Fargo.

Fargo wagged the barrel of the Colt. "I don't chew my cabbage twice, Sancho."

When Fargo thumbed the hammer back, Hachita finally lay the Big Fifty on the floor beside his chair.

"See, jefe?" he said to Lutz. "See why Crawley is dead? Never mind the arrows, his heart was ripped out by a bullet from this one's gun."

"So that's it," Fargo said. "Crawley got his wick snuffed by Apaches last night, but I'm the favorite boy for the crime. Hell, you'd ought to tack up bunting. He was all gurgle and no guts."

Bearcat frowned. "I know he had his limits, but he was a strong right arm to me."

"That's your business. I was hoping to kill him myself, but this way I at least save a bullet."

Lutz's eyes cut to Hachita. "I still need that strong right arm, Fargo. My earlier offer holds. With you as my ramrod, this territory is ripe pickings."

Fargo laughed. "Looks like you don't know whether to string me up or hire me, do you. So tell me, did Crawley dump his poison in the water?"

Bearcat stopped pacing, puzzling that one out. "That's got me treed. Tomorrow morning, early, I need you to ride down there and check. Look here, Fargo."

Like a kid with a new top, Lutz grabbed a letter written on onionskin paper from the desk. "This is a personal endorsement from the editor of the *Santa Fe New Mexican*, reprinted in his paper, supporting my campaign for territorial governor."

Lutz wanted Fargo to take and read it, but the latter ignored it.

"Helps to have the quill drivers on your side," Fargo said civilly, still watching Hachita.

"Damn right, but it can be lost in a heartbeat if we leave an entire Apache clan poisoned for the buzzards. That's why you have to get in there and look around. If it's safe, I'll have my boys come and bury the bodies in a pit. Lime will hold the smell down."

Hachita spoke up, his voice a toneless rasp. "Don't trust this one, Bearcat. He caused the rock slide that killed Hamp, and he killed Crawley and the others last night. He is gelding you."

"You may be right," Lutz conceded without effort. "After all, he spends too much time alone, and such men are dangerous. But a man who's lying to you, Hachita, does not cavalierly tell you he's a liar like Fargo did a couple minutes ago."

"Unless," Hachita cautioned, "he is a fox and knows that you will turn his words to his advantage."

Bearcat shook his head. "With me, such transparent stratagems won't work."

Hachita said, "What kind of gems?"

"Never mind. I'm only saying that if Fargo *is* bamboozling us, he's doing a smooth job of it. Nobody's found any flies on him—not one shred of proof against him. But don't worry—we'll soon sift this matter to the bottom."

To the bottom . . . Fargo didn't like the ominous sound of that. Nor did he believe Lutz had decided to trust him. No man would ever see all of Bearcat Lutz's cards.

Bearcat opened the humidor on his desk and handed Fargo a banded cigar. "Meantime," he said in a voice as phony as his smile, "here's to the newest member of the team."

Fargo bit the end off and planted the cigar in his teeth. He pulled a phosphor from his possibles bag, but it was only halfway to his cigar when an earsplitting snap filled the room. The popper on Hachita's whip streaked toward Fargo. Before he could react, he realized the match in his hand was burning.

"I am even better with the hatchet," Hachita informed him. "No man knows, Fargo, when it is time to take the dirt nap."

"I agree," Fargo told him, meeting his demented gaze. "*No* man."

13

Fargo and Snakeroot hit the desert trail south while the sun was still a dull red ball on the eastern horizon. It was only the fifth day since Fargo arrived in Tucson, yet things were rapidly coming to a head.

"Fargo, this is hog stupid," Snakeroot complained. His face was puffy and creased from lack of sleep. "If you and Eskiminzin already cooked up the plan, why actually ride out to the Apache camp? Just tell Lutz you already checked and the poison worked."

"Snakeroot, you are some piece of work. You're half Apache, and you ask me that? An Apache is trickier than a redheaded woman—I can't assume Eskiminzin will follow the plan."

"Well, the way he fawned all over that stone you showed him, I thought he was going to adopt you. He even quit scowling at me after that. He won't deal from the bottom of the deck with you."

Fargo's lake blue eyes read the terrain for warnings. "I tend to agree, but the Indian is a notional creature. Anyhow, the real danger right now is Lutz. The man is getting desperate, and that makes him more unpredictable."

"You think he'll have us jumped? That damn coffee grinder you wouldn't destroy is still out there."

Fargo shook his head. "No, but this could be a big test—of me. Crawley is dead, and madman Hachita makes Bearcat jumpy."

"He'd make a slug jumpy."

"Yeah, which is why Lutz means it when he says he can't make it without a good ramrod."

"Meaning you?"

"Meaning me," Fargo agreed. "He's desperate, and he's making himself believe he can maybe trust me—or trust my greed. What I do on this ride could be his last big test of me."

"Spies?"

Fargo nodded.

"Plenty of Apache turncoats around here," Snakeroot mused. "They get tossed out of camp by the Apache star chamber, and to get even they work for the white-eyes."

"Yeah, and they could be watching at any point, so it's got to look real."

"You're not *too* stupid," Snakeroot conceded. "But why do you need me along for this trip?"

"*Need* you? Hell, I need you like I need the drizzling squitters. But I want it clear you're my sidekick because I've got a hunch Hachita and the crew are looking to kill you. I'll serve notice to Lutz that he doesn't get me without you."

"*Ya lo veo*—now I see it. The only reason my ass is hanging in the wind is because of teaming up with you in the first place. Now you're going to save me?"

"If everything works out," Fargo said, "you'll be all right."

"In your vast experience with these matters, how often does 'everything' work out?"

"Prac'ly never," Fargo said cheerfully. "Do you think you're going to live forever?"

"Christ, I'd like to make it at least until my next piss."

Fargo grinned. "Go *real* soon, and I'll guarantee it."

"If something does go wrong today, does that mean we go to ground in the jacal?"

"Depends what might go wrong."

Snakeroot hooted, then took yet another swig from his canteen, smacking his lips. Fargo snatched it from his hand and sniffed it.

"Giggle water. I thought so." Fargo emptied it into the sand.

"Hey! I worked two hours for that whiskey."

But as they rode farther from Tucson, Fargo grew silent and followed his usual trail vigilance. Before midmorning the old Spanish water hole edged into view. The two riders climbed the long slope behind it and topped a sandstone ridge. A small, pear-shaped valley opened up below them, dotted with small adobe houses and brush huts once occupied by Mexicans.

"*Hijo,*" Snakeroot whispered at the grim sight below. "You sure it ain't real?"

"No," Fargo admitted. "But deception and trickery are favorite games with the Apache. Draw the Remington."

"Why?"

"Pile on the agony," Fargo muttered in a weary tone as he drew his Colt. "See those surrounding ridges? Remember our talk about possible spies? Don't you think they'd expect you to unlimber until you had a closer look?"

"No need to fart blood about it," Snakeroot groused, pulling the six-shooter from his sash.

At first, Fargo really did fear something had gone horribly wrong. Everywhere the eye looked lay "dead" Apaches, even the well-disciplined children, not twitching a limb. A woman carrying an infant staggered from a hut, and Fargo appeared to viciously gun her down. He also halted the Ovaro a few times to—evidently—shoot at dying Apaches on the ground.

Fargo recognized the muscular Apache who lay facedown in front of a hut. Fargo spoke in a low voice, not looking at the man on the ground. Snakeroot translated in the same manner.

"Be patient, Eskiminzin, I know your people have been out here since dawn. It should be over soon. The spies must be fooled by now."

"We have endured much harder things, Son of Light, and endured them in silence. We will wait for your signal."

Fargo wasn't too worried about the Apaches keeping up the ruse—they were a patient people with the endurance of a doorknob. But a tough job still lay ahead when Fargo made his report to Bearcat. The cards had to fall Fargo's way, or all his big plans turned to mental vapors, and his next bed was an unmarked grave in the sagebrush.

"C'mon," he told Snakeroot. "Time to make my report to the boss."

The moment Fargo entered Bearcat's library, he knew there had been a sea change in Lutz's attitude toward him. The man was all smiles and finally cut the report short.

"Fargo, I'm already a believer. I confess I had spies watching you this morning. When they told me you cut down an Apache woman and her kid, I knew you were straight goods."

"He is tricking you, Bearcat," Hachita said from his favorite wing chair. "Your cowardly spies are too far away to see bullets hit."

Lutz, however, was far too elated to abide such talk.

"You know, Fargo," he said, "Crawley could be a nervous Nellie at times, but he did some good work for me. The truth is, I'm not going to hang on to my empire unless I hire a man of your caliber. Are you interested?"

"I just might be, at that."

Lutz looked like a starving man staring at food. "Excellent! We'll talk more after we take care of cleanup."

"He's sticking it in you," Hachita warned his boss, "and he will break it off inside you."

"Hachita, you're some pumpkins when it comes to torturing and killing. But you're no student of human character."

Lutz looked at Fargo. "As a businessman, naturally I enjoy settling accounts. This incident will get noised about very quickly, but if the bodies are removed, everybody will eventually assume they rode into Old Mexico and got scalped for bounties. So they'll be buried quick."

"Good," Fargo said. "But even with this bunch all dead, a trap could be waiting. There's Mescaleros roving this area, and they could have heard about the mass poisoning—the moccasin telegraph can be quicker than the white man's."

"I forgot about the Messy Apaches. All right, I'll have Hachita round up all my men we can spare. That'll make the burying faster, too."

Fargo felt a great weight lift from his chest. This entire ruse was wasted if not enough men rode out.

"You know," Bearcat mused aloud, "those red devils cost me tens of thousands of dollars. I have to see this with my own eyes."

To keep from smiling, Fargo had to bite the inside of his cheeks until he tasted blood. The more the merrier.

Hachita met Fargo's eyes and seemed to read his thoughts. "*Ojo!* Careful, Bearcat, you're going to regret this. Fargo could sell a glass of water to a fish."

Bearcat waved this aside and sent Fargo a wink. "Fine, don't worry about it, Hachita. You'll be going along, so if Fargo gets out of line, you'll just kill him. Now go round up the men."

Most of the riders formed a long single file, with Fargo, Snakeroot, Bearcat, and Hachita forming a set of four in the vanguard.

Bearcat rode astride a big gray gelding. His mood was effusive and almost jolly.

"You know, Fargo, I'm not one of these men of the 'nits make lice' school. There's room for the Indian out here if he'll just give

104

up his heathen, nomadic ways and harken and heed to the white man's laws. But these bullheaded Apaches . . . sometimes you have to destroy the lawn to kill the crabgrass."

Fargo missed the logic of that last sentence completely, but just nodded. "You bend with the breeze or you break. The Indian refuses to change with the rest of the world."

"What oft was thought, Fargo. What oft was thought."

Fargo sat his saddle in a relaxed but vigilant posture. He and Lutz led the way, with Hachita and Snakeroot riding abreast behind them. About twenty Committeemen followed, some with shovels tucked into their saddle scabbards, their scarred, sore-used horses proof these men lacked warm and beating hearts. But it was Hachita, so close behind his back, who had Fargo on edge.

"Speaking of Apaches," Lutz said, lowering his voice so only Fargo could hear. "Why bring the half-breed along? You killed the last Apache who could talk, didn't you? What's to translate?"

"Eskiminzin's bunch are past talking," Fargo said with confident swagger. "But if we lock horns with Mescaleros, maybe we can buy them off cheap. Apaches will sell a vengeance."

Lutz chuckled. "Fargo, you read them like a book."

Lutz was good at chasing nickels, Fargo thought, but a weak sister when it came to riding skills. All horses sniffed the ground to reassure themselves in new country, but each time his gray tried to do so, Lutz jerked back the reins hard.

"There's the water hole," Bearcat called out, his tone tense with excitement.

Fargo had to be fully alert. He and Eskiminzin had agreed it was best if the Apaches let the stranglers move in close among them before rising up to fight. Yet, at any moment some drunk, trigger-happy vigilante might open up on a "corpse." It was Fargo's job to prevent that.

"Jesus H. Christ on a crutch," one of the stranglers said as the group rode in sight of the bodies. "Crawled outside to die like rats."

"It's money for old rope," Lutz gloated. "Gone-up cases, all of them."

"Why even bury them red sons?" one of his men shouted. "I say give 'em turnabout. Cut their tallywhackers off, shove 'em in their mouths, and just leave the whole bunch for carrion. That's how they do the white man!"

Despite this bravado, the speaker, and several other men, were foolishly picketing their mounts to clumps of sagebrush. Fargo suspected these city greenhorns were about to regret that mistake.

Hachita caught Fargo's eye, baring yellow teeth like crooked gravestones. His voice was a thunderous bellow. "A sea of corpses, eh? We all know that a body dead even a short time will not bleed from new wounds. *Mira!* Watch this!"

He raised his double-ten and aimed at a young woman lying in front of a hut. The moment Fargo's right hand slapped leather, Hachita swung the barrels toward him and fired, the concussion leaving Fargo's ears throbbing like Pawnee war drums. At the same moment, the Ovaro had stutter-stepped nervously. This move spared Fargo's life as most of the shot whistled over his right shoulder.

He was not, however, completely spared as bloody events unfolded with nightmarish speed and confusion. In a wound similar to last night's blast, perhaps a dozen Blue Whistlers, along with heat and flame from the muzzle blasts, slammed Fargo backward out of the saddle. He hit the ground hard on his back, stunned immobile but not unconscious.

For a man of action, it was the ultimate trial. Unable to even twitch a finger, feeling warm blood on his scalp and neck, Fargo watched in impotent horror as Hachita tugged the bone-handle hatchet from his sash, grinning at Fargo. But Fargo's clover was deep today—fate intervened in the form of shrieking Apaches, rising from the weapons hidden beneath them when Hachita's express gun spoke its piece. In an instant the scene went from a murder attempt to a full-blown shooting fray.

By now, Fargo could see, Bearcat Lutz wore a mask of sheer terror. As the Apaches rose up, shrieking their bloodcurdling kill cries, his big gray bucked hard. Lutz managed to hang on, but the Hunt repeating rifle in his saddle boot slid from its sheath and hit the ground, discharging. Lutz screamed like a woman as blood blossomed from his left thigh, and Fargo was convinced it was curtains for this murderer and slaver. Especially with warpath Apaches surging toward him.

But Fargo hadn't counted on Hachita saving Bearcat's bacon. Hachita grabbed Lutz's reins, shouted, "Hang on!" and wheeled his horse and galloped north, bullets snapping all around them.

Fargo had planned on staying out of this fight, but not this way. Only gradually he gained control over his limbs while his head throbbed with pain. Hachita and Bearcat may have escaped, but

Lutz's men were far less fortunate. At the first shrieks from the Apaches, the frightened horses tied to clumps of sagebrush snapped free, stranding their riders, and Apaches overran the screaming enemy like Viking Berserkers.

A few escaped, but soon seventeen men lay dead and mutilated on the battlefield. An elated Eskiminzin reported that only three Apaches had been wounded, none seriously.

Fargo mopped at his bloody but superficial wounds with a neckerchief, then joined Snakeroot in a survey of the carnage.

"I told you it wouldn't come off perfect," Fargo said, "but this is far from a failure, too. After all, almost half of Lutz's criminal army are lying dead in the sand."

"Good riddance. But Lutz got away, and he's got more dirt workers in town."

"That's the way of it," said Fargo. "We have to finish off Lutz before he can regroup and hire new guns."

Snakeroot, still shaken by the brief, violent encounter, watched Apaches looting the bodies and fighting over the horses they could catch.

"These pigs deserved slaughtering long ago," he said. "They shoot old men and cripples for sport, I've seen it. But what about when word gets out?"

"Yeah, what about it? White courts have upheld the Indian's right of self-defense. The heavily armed vigilantes died right here in an Apache stronghold. That spells an illegal raid on the Indians, which it damn sure was, and makes what happened self-defense."

"You sound like an Indian Bureau lawyer. You're not telling me that a white man's court would rule that way?"

Fargo gingerly plucked a shard of buckshot from his scalp. "No, I'm saying that's why the courts don't even care. Adventurers on the frontier are taking well-known risks, especially when facing wild Indians who aren't subject to white man's courts. Besides, who would investigate, and why? Indians have killed hundreds out here in the past year, none of the killings investigated."

"That shines," Snakeroot said. "Far as killing Bearcat, he's got plenty of criminal allies, but not one friend. Ain't one of them crooked shits gonna say a word on his behalf. Hell, they'll be fighting over his whore."

Eskiminzin approached them, and Fargo managed in Spanish, "What about the bodies?"

"Devil's Floor," he replied, and Fargo approved this with a nod.

No bodies, no crimes. This treacherous stretch of desert east of Colossal Cave was regularly avoided by most travelers—a waterless, violent stretch comparable to New Mexico's Jornada del Muerto or Journey of Death. For years no one but Apaches had ranged onto Devil's Floor, and these still-bloody bodies would soon become more bleached bones among plenty of others no one ever gazed on or gave a marker.

"This was a good victory," Fargo opined, "but we didn't cut off the head of the snake. If we wait too long before we strike, our hash is cooked. Let's get Amy out to the hut, then scratch out a plan for the prison raid."

14

After considering the dangers in Tucson, Fargo guessed there was going to be a brief respite in the violence. Lutz would have to see a doctor and get that slug cut out, an operation that might itself kill him if infection set in. Besides, he had just been scared spitless and lost almost half his thugs, and many who remained were needed at the mine and prison.

"Fargo, do you really think she's safer out in the jacal?" Snakeroot asked when the riders, trotting their mounts to spare them in the desert heat, were halfway back to Tucson.

"Use your head, kid. I'd bet my horse Lutz is making plans right now to nab her. Even if he kills her old man, she's a credible witness against Lutz. He realizes, now that his power is threatened, that he could sink fast, and she'll have to disappear."

"Yeah, that makes sense. But like you said, he got scared bad today. Maybe he'll just cut his losses and point his bridle someplace else."

Fargo gave that a skeptical grunt. "Yeah, and oysters can walk upstairs, too. Christ, Snakeroot, does your mother know you're out? Can't you see Lutz is brainsick when it comes to money? I'd wager he ain't about to show us any quarter, and that's why we're going to stay on him like ugly on a vulture."

They rode in silence for ten more minutes.

"Borrow your canteen?" Snakeroot spoke up. "I'm spittin' cotton."

"Hell yes you are," Fargo said, tossing his canteen to Snakeroot. "Wha'd'you expect when you fill your canteen with who-shot-John instead of water?"

"Hell, I'm a drunk, not a frontiersman."

In town, they made a quick stop to stock up on oats at the livery. Fargo had already paid a deposit on the mule and now paid for three more days' rental. They rode to Amy's house, Fargo's methodical eyes missing nothing, and hitched at the common rail on the plaza. Fargo gave the prearranged knock.

"Skye! You're hurt again in the same place!" she exclaimed after opening the door.

"Yeah, the blood's a dead giveaway, isn't it?" Fargo remarked, his tone more teasing than sarcastic. "Don't worry. That wound's a long way from my heart."

"I'm surprised that hard head of yours is even vulnerable."

She led him inside and began cleaning him up, Snakeroot bolting the door and standing guard at the window within earshot.

"Today was the second part of your water hole trick, wasn't it?" she asked.

"It was, and it didn't work out too bad. But Lutz knows for sure now that I'm his worst enemy, and that means the three of us have to leave town right now."

"And my father?" she asked, forgetting to breathe.

"A group of Apache warriors will rendezvous with me and Snakeroot just before dawn. We're launching a sunrise raid on the prison."

Amy had to suddenly sit down. "But what if Bearcat's men simply kill Father and the others at the first sound of attack?"

Fargo shrugged. "Then they kill him. We're in no position to be wet-nursin' him or any other prisoner. They plan to kill him anyway, so a surprise raid is his best chance."

"Yes," she said decisively. She stood up and crossed to a canvas bag on a nearby chair. "I knew this was coming. That's why I dressed for travel."

Fargo and Snakeroot exchanged quick grins. Her idea of dressing for a rough outing was a simple blue gingham dress and a starched-white bonnet—more appropriate for picking berries, Fargo thought.

She opened the drawstring bag to tuck in a few yellowish lumps of lye-and-tallow soap.

"Where will I bathe?" she asked hesitantly. "Or . . . *will* I bathe?"

"There's a feeder creek close by," Fargo replied.

"One of us should be with you, though," Snakeroot said. "For safety," he hastily added.

"I packed my Colt Navy," she assured him, her tone implying he'd damn well better remember the fact.

"Speaking of safety," Fargo said, "let's put Tuscon behind us before Lutz knows we're here."

Amy gave the house a long, parting glance, bravely fighting back tears as she realized she might never see it again. Fargo tied her bag to the mule's rigging, then reached down to pull Amy up so she could ride postilion with him. Fargo left Tucson to the west, Amy clinging tightly, then doubled back around to the east and the small brush canyon.

The western sky was a rosy flush by the time they picked their way down into the canyon and reached the well-hidden jacal. Amy stared around her at the cactus and creosote brush, a cruel parody of the green Lake Erie forests where she grew up.

"This isn't Fiddler's Green," Fargo apologized as he helped her down. "But you'll be safer here. There's room to swing a cat in. We can see any visitors approaching by day, and it's too hard a ride at night."

"My goodness," Amy fussed, both hands smoothing her dress. "My clothes need what my Aunt Thelma calls 'a good pull-down.'"

Evidently, Snakeroot misinterpreted Aunt Thelma's meaning. "Pull them down as far as you'd like," he invited Amy. "We won't be offended."

She gave him a strained smile. "How gallant of both of you."

Fargo laughed. "Oh, this is gonna be some cozy little family. Snakeroot, like I said, you don't have to speak every thought that enters your head. Launder your speech for the lady."

"All right, Don Juan, *you* tell her we didn't have time to dig a jakes, either. Tell her that all of nature is at her disposal."

"I already assumed that," she said archly. "I'm not a princess."

"Pretty as one, though," Snakeroot said, charming a smile out of her.

Fargo cleared his throat. "If you two are done billing and cooing . . . now, the food we have on hand will hold us a few days. If we have to stay any length of time, we'll have meat. There's ground-nesting birds all around—plenty of scaled quail and prairie chickens. If you cook—he kicked at a pile of dead mesquite and cottonwood chunks he'd gathered up last time out—deadwood doesn't smoke, so that's all we'll burn."

"Let's eat and turn in," Snakeroot suggested. "I could sleep standing up."

"You can eat, and you can sleep two hours," Fargo told him. "Enough time to rest our mounts. Then you and me are riding back to Tucson."

"Fargo, you're crazy as a shitepoke! We got a battle tomorrow at dawn."

"So I've heard. That's why we're riding back to Tucson."

Bearcat Lutz supported himself on a rattan cane, his face pale and nervous—highly unusual for him, Yet, he was still able to pace up and down his showcase library, expounding to anyone who would listen about his grandiose plans to become a Western potentate.

"Gents, add a little skill to a lot of luck, and what do you get? You get *fame*. You get Skye Goddamn Fargo, that's what."

He looked at Hachita, who was sprawled negligently in a wing chair eating an apple. "Did you see it, Hachita? Fargo's stallion crow-hopped just as you fired. Even his damn horse is a dime-novel hero."

Hachita wiped his mouth on his sleeve. "What's all the whoop-de-doo, Bearcat? Fargo ain't going anywhere just yet. That *maldito* means to free the prisoners, and he won't let much grass grow under his feet before he tries. And I'd wager Eskiminzin and his best warriors will be siding Fargo."

"That's one wager I'm refusing," Lutz conceded, his tone bitter. "That son of a bitch Fargo has been one step ahead of me since he rode into Tucson less than a week ago. He's even got Amy Hanchon into hiding somewhere—I sent Dan and Jorge to her house to seize her, but she'd lit out."

"She'll turn up," Hachita predicted. "And when she does, remember you don't need two night women. You got Lupita."

Lutz ignored this and turned to the third man in the room, Sam Ulrick. He was middle-aged and paunchy, but prosperous-looking in a silk vest with a gold watch chain looping from the fob pocket to a buttonhole.

"Sam, is it true you bought a private treaty with Eskiminzin?"

"Half true. Bearcat, any whiskey trader has a private treaty with wild Indians. Without me, there is no crazy water. They won't kill me unless my price is too high, and I make sure it never is."

"I've seen drunk Indians," Lutz said. "Drunk soldiers are death to the devil, but a redskin? I watched one pull a burning stick from a fire and set his own hair ablaze. If those Apaches get all jollified tonight, they'll be useless for two days. That should buy me and Hachita enough time to recruit new men."

"At least two days," Ulrick agreed. "But even a private treaty can't guarantee my safety when Apaches are greased for war. And don't forget the penalty for selling whiskey to hostile Indians has risen from a stiff fine to hanging."

"Penalty? Sell your ass! There's no authority left out here to impose any penalty. Hell, I'm the law. But go ahead, let's hear your terms."

"Tell you what," Ulrick said. "You pay me wholesale for the whiskey and add one hundred dollars for my risk and trouble."

Lutz's right thumb and forefinger stroked his goatee. "Hmm . . . that seems suspiciously cheap. Why?"

"Just remember me after you're elected, all right? I'm switching to legitimate freight hauling, and government contracts will flow across your desk."

Lutz grinned, flattered. "Hitch your wagon to a star, huh? Damn straight I'll remember you, Sam. Now you better get humping with that whiskey."

Ulrick shrugged into a velvet-trimmed topcoat while Lutz added: "Spread the word, Sam, that I'm paying top dollar for gunmen. I'm damned if I'm tossing years of hard work right down a rat hole without fighting. Skye God Almighty Fargo was worthless during the fighting today—hell, even that half-breed got a few rounds off. I'll turn that frontier legend into a national joke."

Fargo and Snakeroot rode out of the brush canyon after dark, bearing southwest so they could enter Tucson from its quiet side.

"I knew you asked me about that powder magazine for a reason," Snakeroot said. "Fargo, *por dios*, that's the crowded part of town. If we blow their powder and ammo up, we could kill half of Tucson."

"That's good if we get the right half. But don't worry. If we stupidly blow it up," Fargo said, "we'll also be giving them time to scare up more ammo. So instead of blowing it, we're gonna . . . compromise it, you might say. With luck, these amateurs won't know it until it's too late."

As he rode, Fargo gnawed on an especially leathery hunk of

buffalo jerky. He promised himself that if he survived this Tucson scrape, he'd find some place that served cornpone and back ribs.

Snakeroot started to speak, but Fargo raised a hand to silence him when the Ovaro's ears pricked forward.

Fargo listened for a full minute, frontier-honed ears sorting out the various sounds that hid behind silence.

"There's a conveyance out there," he said. "I can hear the tug chains."

Using his hearing to guide them, Fargo and Snakeroot rode south for perhaps ten minutes and almost collided with a somber black carriage trimmed in silver, its two coal-oil running lights showing a roof decorated with feather plumes. Only when Fargo spotted the oval viewing window on the side did he realize what it was.

"Hell's bells!" Fargo said in astonishment. "It's a hearse."

"Sam Ulrick's hearse," Snakeroot supplied. "He's the undertaker in Tucson."

"Tell me," Fargo said as they rode closer, "does he drink at the Sagebrush or the Black Bear?"

"I take your drift about his loyalties, but he's a teetotaler. He's been known, though, to sell liquor to Indians, so he's in Bearcat's camp."

Fargo followed the rule of frontier etiquette and gave Ulrick a hail, asking for permission to approach.

"Whoever you are, friend, come closer. I can't see past the glare of my lanterns."

"Well, I can, so keep your hands where they are right now."

Fargo saw a sumptuously dressed man in a plug hat, squinting in the darkness to see them.

"Jesus, Sam," Snakeroot greeted him, "the hell you doing out here, especially after dark?"

"Duty calls, gentlemen. Sad duty. I'm taking the body of a young man back to his family in Albuquerque. I travel at night to spare the horses."

"All that makes some sense, but that corpse wagon of yours ain't even thorough-braced for long distances," Fargo pointed out. "You'd bust both axles in the badlands."

"See here, friend, do you have some authority in this matter? Are you a federal marshal? I protest this—"

"Sew up your lips," Fargo snapped. "I'm asking the questions. If you're making a long trip, where's your food and water? There ain't one real settlement between here and Albuquerque."

"As to that . . . you see . . . that is, it would seem—"

"You say," Fargo cut in, "you're hauling a body across hundreds of miles of rough desert. Gonna smell kind of ripe, ain't it?"

"Well, of course, the dearly departed has been packed in salt to preserve him."

"Mind if we look in the back?" Fargo asked.

"Help yourself, you'll find all is in order. Door's unlocked."

First Fargo thrust a hand into Ulrick's coat pocket and came out with a small revolver.

"Colt Pocket Model," Fargo said. "Good gun. I'll hold it until we leave."

He moved behind the hearse and threw open the double doors, then grabbed one of the running lamps off its mount and thrust it inside.

Snakeroot whistled. "Looks like he's on the level with us. Ain't nothing else back here but that."

"That" was a large pine coffin that had been sanded and finished. A lock secured the lid.

"Just like I thought," Fargo said. "The bastard's in a perfect profession to be a whiskey peddler."

"Fargo, you couldn't get enough bottles of fire water in that one coffin to make the risk worthwhile."

"I've seen this same setup in the Utah Territory, too. Look how deep the wheels are cutting into the sand. One body isn't that heavy. Ulrick doesn't need bottles—I'll wager that coffin is lined with tin and has a cork seal around the lid to block the smell. The whiskey is piped right into it. Respect for the dead keeps even lawmen from looking too close. One coffin can get an entire red nation drunk as the lords of creation."

Snakeroot made a farting noise with his lips. "*Vaya*, Fargo, I better put my boots on—it's getting deep. A coffin lined with tin? You must think I just fell off the turnip wagon."

Fargo went around front and invited Ulrick, at gun point, to open the coffin.

"Gentlemen," he sputtered, "this is an outrage. I am being violated."

"Shut pan and open that coffin," Fargo said. "Or give me the key."

The moment the cork-sealed lid went up, a strong smell of mash filled the hearse. Whiskey shimmered in the coffin.

"*Hijo!* Tin lining just like you said," Snakeroot marveled.

"Bearcat had a wingding planned for Eskiminzin's bunch, didn't he?" Fargo asked Ulrick.

Ulrick shrugged. "Something along those lines, I suppose."

"Give me a hand dumping this Indian burner," Fargo told Snakeroot, starting to wrestle the heavy coffin out.

"Gentlemen, might forty dollars in gold eagles dissuade you from this wasteful course?" Ulrick wheedled.

"Mister, you're damn lucky if we don't shoot you. The penalty for peddling whiskey to Indians is death by hanging, and there's a damn good reason for that. The blood of innocent women and children is on your hands."

"That is preposterous, sir. I am simply a merchant supplying a need."

"Keep pushing it, poncy man," Fargo warned.

Ulrick wisely fell silent and put on his best mourning face.

"This bitch is heavy," Snakeroot grunted as they set the coffin down on the desert floor. Fargo's lariat-tough muscles strained as he tipped it over, the dry, thirsty desert sand soaking up the liquor almost instantly.

"This is high-handed behavior," Ulrick complained, albeit mildly.

Fargo swung up into leather. "You think this is bad, whiskey runner? Wait until the next time I catch you assisting Bearcat's filthy plans. You'll learn exactly how a rooster is turned into a capon."

Fargo was grateful for the inky shadows of nighttime Tucson, where a complete lack of streetlamps favored stealthy movement. He and Snakeroot tethered their mounts in an alfalfa field and slipped into town like a pair of thieves.

"There's likely to be guards on that powder magazine," Snakeroot said, still trying to talk Fargo out of this brazen madness.

"Not likely. This is a cocky bunch, and having the Sagebrush right next door makes them even cockier. Who would dare cross them so nearby?"

"Still . . . Fargo, we're bearding the lion."

"Even lions require barbers. Remember, I'm not doing this for sport," Fargo assured him. "Eskiminzin and his warriors will feel duty-bound, since they're helping Son of Light, to be courageous in this fight. They'll attack into the teeth of the enemy, and I owe it to those Apaches to keep their casualties low. This is the best way I know how."

"That rings right," Snakeroot surrendered. "There's two windows in the back, both boarded up, but we can't get to 'em except from the front—at the rear, the approaches are all blocked by buildings."

They rounded a shadowy corner of the plaza, and Fargo could make out the fronts of three buildings: Lutz's house, the Sagebrush Saloon, and the boarded-up dance hall whose rear half was the stranglers' powder magazine.

"Damn it all," Fargo cursed quietly. "I was right—no guards except one in front of Bearcat's place. But look at *that* pair, wouldja?"

Fargo meant the *nymphs du pave* who had parked their gaudy, feathered frames right in front of the old dance hall.

"Hell, that's Socorro and Lupe," Snakeroot said. "They use to belong to the stable of whores at the Black Bear. They got caught knocking down—you know, turning in less money than they earned. Now they're on their own."

"You know 'em?"

"In the Old Testament sense," Snakeroot boasted. "This one time? I dressed Socorro up like Joan of—"

"Never mind the disgusting brags," Fargo snapped. "Take this and get them the hell out of there. But be careful to avoid lights."

He handed Snakeroot several silver pesos. The mixed-breed approached the women, spoke with them a few moments, then handed them the money. The demimonde divas then moved down the plaza, and Fargo hurried forward.

The two men moved to the rear. Thanks to the serious shortage of nails out West, the boards were only loosely nailed up. Fargo's Arkansas Toothpick was easily up to the task of prying them loose.

"I'll boost you in first," Fargo said, "but for Christ sakes, don't light any matches until we know where the powder kegs are, or we could be blown to smithereens."

Fargo easily lifted Snakeroot over the sill, then rolled in behind him. Interior walls blocked this back room from the plaza, and Fargo knew a weak light wouldn't be visible. He pulled a stub of candle from his possibles bag, then thumb-scratched a lucifer to life and lit it.

Everywhere he looked, plaster had cracked and fallen, exposing the lathing beneath.

"There," Fargo said. "Against the back wall."

"*Por dios!* They could kill every man, woman, child, and coyote in the Arizona Territory."

Fargo had to agree. The Gatling gun sat on its heavy tripod, ammunition hopper filled to the brim. Four wooden kegs of gunpowder sat beside it. Gun racks on the wall above the powder kegs held carbines, repeating rifles, a few more of the sawed-off express guns. Shelves held cartons of cartridges.

"Shit, I'm stealing one of these rifles," Snakeroot vowed.

"Like hell you are. That'll tip them we were here, and they'll likely inspect everything. Here, take this."

Fargo handed him a curved horseshoe nail, then grabbed a carbine off the rack.

"Watch me," he said. "You just stick one end of the nail under the firing pin—here—and bend until you hear it click, like that. Now it's disabled, but only an armory expert could spot it at a glance."

"All the saints," Snakeroot gloated, grabbing another carbine. "These stupid sons of bitches will end up with nothing but their dicks in their hands."

"Don't bury them just yet, skinny. These are most likely spare weapons and ammo they won't have to use tomorrow."

"Not that Gatling."

"Not that unless they have two," Fargo agreed. "And they're planning a high old time with it, so I hope this is the only gun."

Before Fargo turned to the Gatling, he pried the bung out of every powder keg, then poured in water from the two canteens he'd brought—not much was required, just enough to "clump" the powder and render it useless. While Snakeroot continued ruining firing pins, Fargo opened each box of cartridges and poured a few drops of neat's-foot oil into each one.

"The hell's that doing?" Snakeroot asked.

"This oil is usually for waterproofing," Fargo explained. "When you put it on metal cartridges, it can't be felt to the touch, but they get slippery when heated and jam in the ejector port. Each one has to be wiped off."

As a final touch, Fargo bent the firing pin on the Gatling. "There. Even if all this doesn't help us much tomorrow, we've made sure their firepower is reduced for the near future. Now let's light a shuck back to the hut and grab some sleep. We've got Apaches to meet at dawn."

"This must finally be it," Reverend Daniel Hanchon said. "Pass the word down the cells: It's coming very soon, be ready."

Hanchon and several other prisoners lay in the filthy straw of their cell, spying through cracks between the adobe bricks. Bearcat Lutz stood nearby, conferring intensely with the prison guards.

"Looks like Hachita is Bearcat's favorite boy now," a balding man named Linton McCallister, lying alongside the reverend, remarked. "Something happened to Crawley."

"Yeah," said the third man who was peering outside, "and I bet that something is named Skye Fargo."

"Yes, it's Fargo," Hanchon said confidently. "But he'll be up against long odds, and he'll need our help. We must all be prepared to—how did Fargo put it?—seize the main chance."

"Say," McCallister said fervently, "I'd run in front of hot lead any day if it means a chance to get out of here."

"From your lips to God's ears," Hanchon said. "Our freedom, our prosperity—"

The third man hissed him quiet. "Oh, hell, they're headed this way. Pretend to be sleeping, boys."

Hanchon lay with his eyes closed and his heart pounding. The front door groaned open, a lamp was lighted, and Hanchon heard scuffling feet stop right outside his cell.

"No point to the charade, Reverend," Bearcat Lutz's voice scraped down his spine. "I know you're awake. And now, soul saver, it's time for a reckoning."

15

Fargo stripped the leather from the Ovaro and watered him from his hat, then dug the army binoculars from a saddle pocket and studied the mine and prison under the new day's pearl gray sky.

"Are they up there?" Snakeroot asked, his voice tight with nervousness.

"In all their charm and glory," Fargo replied. "Led by the Hatchet. The Gatling's in place, too."

Assuming this was the same gun, Fargo figured that sometime during the night the Gatling had been hauled to a good vantage point near the assay shack, where it could be swiveled to cover any slope.

"Wait till they figure out that gun ain't worth an old underwear button," Snakeroot said.

"*If* that's the same gun we broke last night. I wouldn't make that assumption. You'll fight harder if you expect the worst."

"The worst," Snakeroot said, "would be to get killed or crippled. What, you got second thoughts about the Apaches?"

Fargo turned to survey their battle allies. About twenty well-muscled braves knelt in the rock declivity, checking their weapons or stuffing their knee-length moccasins with sage grass to soften stones on the slope. Anticipating hand-to-hand combat, some of the braves wore heavy copper brassards to protect their vulnerable upper arms.

"I can't give a cast-iron guarantee about the Apaches," Fargo replied. "Every tribe I've ever met is unwilling to take heavy casualties. I won't sugarcoat it, Snakeroot—if those Apaches abandon the field with us topside, we'll be in a world of hurt."

"*De veras.* And if that damn ghoul Sam Ulrick had got through last night, these braves would all be unmanned by strong water. That Lutz is what you call a resourceful son of a bitch."

"Evidently he's also a coward," Fargo said. "All the old, familiar faces are up there except his—conspicuously, but not surprisingly, absent."

"Lutz? Why *should* he be there? He doesn't know beans from buckshot about fighting. He hires out all his killing."

"Well, the Hatchet knows plenty about fighting. Matter fact, he's too battle savvy to count on any one weapon. Behind the Gatling he's got a line of about ten riflemen in a shallow trench. And about half that number appear to be roving skirmishers, free to flow with the battle. Like we'll be doing."

"Is Hachita's defense smart?"

"Against Indians I'd've done it that way myself."

Snakeroot didn't like the sound of this. "Fargo, that's high ground. You don't have to sit on the benches at West Point to know high ground is the hardest to take."

"And the hardest to *hold* if they panic, and that's our job—make them panic. Just nerve up."

"Yeah, that's what I'll do. Nerve up. There, it's done. Jesus, Fargo, you're a caution."

Eskiminzin, his face leather tough from long exposure to desert sun, approached the two men. His scarred chest and arms, pocked by burns and knife scars and old bullet wounds, told the violent history of his life in the West.

"Are you ready?" Fargo asked him in Spanish.

"We are not here to discuss the causes of the wind," Eskiminzin assured him through Snakeroot. "We came to kill this spawn of the Wendigo."

Eskiminzin paused to look through Fargo's binoculars. "This Lutz. This many-headed snake, he came here calling himself our brother and speaking honeyed words about the People. When he realized his trinkets could not make us leave this land, he decided to wipe all of us out."

And then even tried to do it with open contempt, Fargo reflected, because there was no authority to stop him. The decreasing number of soldiers at Camp Grant were kept on coffee-cooling detail while violence swept through the Arizona Territory like a grass fire. Eskiminzin was right about Lutz, but the Apaches, too, were ruthless marauders—an observation Fargo wisely kept to himself.

"Soon," Eskiminzin said, "new death wickiups will be built, and the names of our dead will never again be spoken. These white-eyes and Mexicans on the hill are braggarts and liars, but words are cheap coins spent freely by toothless old women. The hair-face pony soldiers can sometimes fight, but these men above us are murderers, not warriors. They brag with words. The Apache brags with weapons."

He suddenly thrust out his red-streamered lance, and it took Fargo a few moments to realize—those were not scalps dangling from it, but cured human faces like many-wrinkled masks. For all the Apache's fierce bravado, however, Fargo did not share Eskiminzin's dismissive opinion of Bearcat's vigilantes. Most of them could neither cipher nor write, but some knew the science of killing.

"We have a present for the white-eyes on that hill," Eskiminzin added, pulling an arrow from his fox-skin quiver and handing it to Fargo. "Each of us has a few of these."

"Is that arrow point made of metal?" Snakeroot asked Fargo.

"Yeah, it's tipped in white man's sheet iron. They clinch damn hard when they strike bone, and a lot of times, even with minor wounds, the victim bleeds out because the point can't be removed in time."

Fargo handed the arrow back while Eskiminzin studied Snakeroot with a skeptical eye. "Is this runt going into battle beside you, Son of Light?" he asked, Snakeroot scowling as he translated.

"Looks like it," Fargo said. "Good thing he's an orphan."

Eskiminzin studied the translator again. "Perhaps he is more Apache than he is Mexican although he looks like a soaked weasel. I was sure that, when the fight came, he would be with the girls in their sewing lodge."

"They'll be women when I leave," Snakeroot said in English for Fargo's benefit. "I got a name to live up to."

"Yessir, a joker in every deck," Fargo said. "This is an Apache headman, you fool, and he likely knows some English. Just stick to what me and Eskiminzin say and don't poke your oar into our boat."

Fargo looked at the Apache. "Eskiminzin, it's time to move out. Snakeroot and I will leave first and go up the back slope. When the sun moves the width of two lodge poles, start your attack."

Eskiminzin nodded.

Fargo looked at Snakeroot. "All right, compadre," he said, sliding his Henry from its boot. "Let's waltz it to 'em."

Fargo had already blazed this path days earlier, and both men made good time crossing from the rock declivity to the back slope Fargo had climbed once before. The Trailsman often memorized landscape instead of word directions, and he remembered the places to avoid and the stretches with the best cover. In only about fifteen minutes, they were near the top.

Fargo tugged Snakeroot under an overhang of rock. "We'll wait here until the Apaches attack."

"What the hell we doin'?" Snakeroot demanded. "I'm just following you like a pup on your heels."

"In fancy terms, it's a two-prong diversion attack. We want Lutz's hangmen trapped between the sap and the bark. The Apaches moving up the easier front slope is the diversion. The main objective, our job, is to kill Hachita because he's the most dangerous. That might even bring the rest to Jesus. Then we bust out those prisoners."

Snakeroot nodded. "Now I see it better. But what's my part in it?"

"You'll be needed, and you'll recognize the moment. When it comes, don't hesitate to debate, just act."

"*Hijo!* You talk like a Gypsy fortune-teller. I need—"

"Need a cat's tail. See this?" Fargo slapped the Volcanic rifle slung over Snakeroot's left shoulder. "And I've got my Henry with a spare loaded magazine. Stick close to me and do exactly what I tell you. Together we can get off sixty-two shots as quick as we can lever, and we'll still have our short guns. Remember that, and don't go puny if we're rushed."

"Fargo, I'm not sure I can do this."

"I *know* you can. And today you're going to be a hero."

Snakeroot looked baffled. "Hell, how can you know that?"

"I knew it that first day on the plaza, when you hot-jawed me even though you thought I was one of Lutz's gunslicks. I knew then and there you were going to side me in this fight. Oh, you were wiping your ass with both hands when brains were passed out, but you've got a set of stones on you."

"Hell, Fargo, I didn't know—"

"Whack the cork," Fargo ordered as he started up the slope again. "We ain't bunkmates. I'm just telling you how it is."

Fargo had guessed it right. He hadn't advanced ten steps before a piercing war cry rose from the desert below. The Apaches were out of sight from the back slope, but the hidebound killers on the crown of the hill saw them plain enough. So many rifles detonated at once that the barrage sounded like an ice floe breaking up.

Snakeroot was breathing hard to keep up with Fargo's much longer legs. "Damn, them stranglers are really pouring it to them," he said. "And the Apaches ain't shooting back."

"They will. They're notorious bullet hoarders and don't shoot until targets are assured. Stick with me."

Fargo ran in a crouch until he could see two of the roving skirmishers, both kneeling as they made it hot for the Apaches charging the front slope. He swung his Henry up to the ready, dropped a bead on the nearest one, and turned the side of his head into a red smear.

Fargo rapidly levered and shot the second man in the neck, levered again and fired, sending the man to Judgment with a clean head shot. The hammering gunfire from the battle covered the sound of Fargo's shots.

"Corey!" Hachita's toneless voice bellowed from somewhere on Fargo's left. "What is wrong, '*mano*? Work that damn coffee grinder!"

"Son of a bitch *won't* work," a frustrated voice shouted back. "The ammo feeds from the hopper, but the damn thing won't fire."

"Bastard Fargo," Hachita cursed, and just then Fargo spotted him near the headframe of the mine. "Keep trying."

Fargo and Snakeroot exchanged grins. Their work last night had not been a total waste. The Hatchet resumed firing with the same Sharps Big Fifty Fargo had seen him cleaning in Bearcat's library.

"Can't you pop that piece of shit over right now?" Snakeroot asked.

"I'm tempted. But we're trying to put the fear of God into the stranglers. Just killing him this way, like it was a random bullet in combat, means he'll die a criminal legend in these parts and inspire more crime. I want his dying to be a warning to the other murderers, rapists, whiskey peddlers, claim jumpers, and assorted riffraff around here."

Fargo saw a third roving skirmisher, at the brim of the front slope, making his carbine smoke as he fired on the Apaches. Fargo sent a bullet into his side, throwing him into a hard tumble all the way down.

Hachita saw the skirmisher tumble, but the man could have tripped or been shot by his own side. The Mexican continued his methodical routine with the potent rifle. He fired, rolled to his side, ejected a spent cartridge, and inserted a fresh one in the breech. Now and then he raised the sight vane as the Apaches drew closer.

"Shouldn't we be doing something?" Snakeroot fretted, hunched down behind a clutch of weeds. "The Apaches must be taking plenty of casualties."

"Not likely," Fargo said. "These men aren't marksmen, and an Apache rarely gives his enemy a target. But you're right—let's open up on that rifle trench even though the Apaches ain't topside yet."

Both men raised from cover and drew a bead. "Put at 'em!" Fargo ordered, squeezing off his first round.

Both rifles took turns barking as the men directed a lethal storm of lead at the stranglers. Hachita finally spotted them and threw down his Sharps, picking up a Cavalry carbine and peppering their position. The two remaining rovers also opened up on them.

"Pull foot!" Fargo shouted as the first spiraling plumes of dust kicked up all around them.

The point was to stay in motion, keep the fight everywhere and the enemy rattled. Surprise, mystify, confuse . . . Fargo led Snakeroot around the crown of the hill until they reached the safety of an ore car. Fargo could hear the Apaches coming up the front slope, making enough racket to wake snakes.

He spotted the man still trying to make the Gatling work.

"It's time to kiss the mistress," Fargo said, laying his right cheek along the Henry's stock. The rifle bucked, the gunner crumpled like a cloth sack, and Fargo swung his muzzle toward the rifle trench again.

"I hear those Apaches getting closer," he told Snakeroot. "Should get interesting when they make it up here."

"I just hope those featherheads stick it out," Snakeroot said. "I'd like to *walk* off this hill."

Fargo knew that most Indians weren't suited for a military-style assault on a well-positioned enemy. But northwest of here, in the Pyramid Lake Uprising that killed hundreds, the Washoe tribe had slain more than 80 percent of their white enemies in an assault much like this one.

"They'll stick," he predicted. "They've fought the dons, the

Mexers, the whites, and damn near every Indian tribe they've ever encountered. They've borrowed the best fighting tricks from every enemy. Now, stow the chin music, and let's make some widows."

Again they poured lead into the trench, taking pressure off the Apaches. Fargo was just emptying his magazine when a booming report from behind sent a giant slug ripping through the ore car. Fargo's moment of stunned immobility passed in a blink, and the will to live instinctively asserted itself.

"Cover down!" he shouted to Snakeroot. "It's Hachita. The cunning bastard nosed us out."

"Fargo!" the killer shouted. "Which one has the sweetest poon—Amy Hanchon or Lupita?"

"You topped Lupita?" Snakeroot demanded. "You lucky bastard, you never told me—"

"Shut pan, knucklehead."

A round came whiffing past Fargo. He raised his voice. "Hachita, you're tossin' a wide loop these days. How you like licking a white man's ass, proud son of Montezuma?"

"That remark will cost you your tongue before I kill you."

"Yeah, you've already made your brags," Fargo reminded him. "Now it's time to kill me."

Fargo had ducked behind a basalt fragment. The Sharps whip-cracked, and a fist-size chunk twirled away.

Fargo knew exactly how long it took Hachita to reload the single-shot Sharps. He charged straight at the headframe and Hachita's position, clearing leather and cocking his Colt. Hachita, glancing up from reloading to see Fargo bearing down on him like destiny, leeched pale.

No way in hell, Fargo knew, could a running man hope for accuracy from a six-gun. But he only needed to get close enough for one good shot, so he started squeezing off rounds to keep Hachita rattled. It worked, but Fargo had lost track of those two roving skirmishers, and at his third shot they opened up on him, trapping him in a deadly cross fire.

Snakeroot recklessly exposed himself to fire, swinging his rifle muzzle between the two rovers. His marksmanship was pathetic, but Fargo didn't care—the fast and scrappy Volcanic had sent them ducking to cover.

Unfortunately, Hachita, too, had ducked to a new location. But Fargo couldn't look for him at the moment—he could see the vanguard of the Apaches, about to top the slope, and the riflemen in the trench on the verge of blind panic. He joined Snakeroot.

"Look!" the copper-tinted mixed-breed exalted. "Looks like you were right, Fargo!"

Several of the men were cussing and throwing down their weapons. A stack of replacement firearms had been left in case any man's barrel overheated. Replacements, Fargo realized, that he and Snakeroot had ruined.

"They're about to break," Fargo said. "Just let 'em go, the Apaches will rope 'em down. We—oh, shit."

Snakeroot followed Fargo's eyes and looked up to the ridge behind them. Flames licked from the prison. Both men heard the muffled cries of men inside, crying for help. Earlier, the prison guards must have joined the fight down here, leaving the prisoners locked in.

"This is your moment, Snakeroot!" Fargo shouted. "The Apaches will finish off this bunch below. Follow me!"

As they scrabbled up the slope toward the plateau above, screams rising up behind them as the stranglers were slaughtered, Fargo kept a wary eye out for Hachita. He was nearly convinced the Hatchet had set this fire, as a diversion, on Lutz's order if the fight went bad. Or he could have done it on his own to cover his escape. If so, the trick had worked.

"*Hijo!*" Snakeroot cursed when they gained the ridge and got a closer look at the fire. "Look at that *chingada* door. Split slabs with an iron lock. No windows, only small vents. And that ring of pointed stakes . . . Look! The roof has caught fire! We can never get to them in time."

The screams from inside stiffened the hair on Fargo's arms, but he stayed frosty and cast a quick glance around them. To clear the work site below, the ore muckers had begun hauling tailings up here. A high-piled ore wagon had been left near a pile of tailings—on an incline, Fargo noted, that led directly to the prison door.

"Let's go," he told Snakeroot, racing up toward the wagon. Fargo had an excellent view of the battle below, where the pitiless Apaches had emerged triumphant. He saw Eskiminzin run his spear through a strangler, then use a stone skull-cracker to cave in his head like a melon.

"Climb onto the wagon after we get it rolling," Fargo ordered as he kicked the chocks from under the rear wheels. "And for Christ sakes, jump when I say to."

Despite the incline, the wagon required hard pushing to get it in motion. Fargo leaped onto the ore tailings and had to tug Snakeroot up by his shirt.

"Maldita!" the mixed-breed cursed. "Here comes them stakes!"

The rumbling, bouncing car smashed into the palisade and sent it flying in shards and splinters. Unfortunately, it also sent the ore wagon veering to the left.

"We're veering off course, Fargo!"

If that happened, Fargo knew, every man in that prison would likely die horribly—and take his testimony against Lutz to the grave, just as Bearcat hoped would happen. In desperation, Fargo grabbed onto one side of the wagon and hung his right leg down. The wagon was veering left, so Fargo hoped that enough drag on the right wheel might correct their course.

He was almost shaken off the wildly jouncing wagon, but managed to ease the sole of his right boot against the iron tire and push back hard, then harder still. Heat flooded the sole of his boot, feeling like glowing coals in mere seconds. But Fargo took the pain and pressed even harder, knowing that for these helpless prisoners, this was their last chance.

"Ay, Chihuahua!" Snakeroot shouted. "She's going back on course, Fargo! You always have to upset the cart, don't you?"

"A joker in every deck," Fargo muttered through clenched teeth, though he admired the kid's spunk under pressure.

Just as they passed the halfway point, however, still picking up speed and Fargo's boot leather smelling like a fresh-branded hide, gunfire erupted from very nearby. Snakeroot cried out when a bullet grazed his right cheek and left a bloody furrow a quarter-inch deep.

Fargo struggled, in his awkward position, to look around them. Then he realized his mistake: Two prison guards had been left up here, and they were crouching behind either front corner of the prison, blasting away at the exposed men on the wagon.

"Take the one on the left!" Fargo shouted, aiming three quick shots at his man and sending him to cover. Only seconds later Fargo roared, "Jump!" Both men sailed off just before the ore-laden wagon caromed into the door, ripping it off its hinges.

Fearing those lurking guards, Fargo sent Snakeroot into the billowing smoke while he flushed out the guards. The moment Fargo rounded a corner, one sprang up from behind a granite boulder, but before he got a shot off, Fargo's slug tore off the crown of his head.

"Fargo!" came Snakeroot's desperate voice from behind him. "There's separate cells inside, and we need the keys!"

Fargo had expected a barracks, not cell blocks. Moving fast and efficiently, keeping an eye out for that missing guard, Fargo quickly searched the dead one for keys.

"Jesus Christ and various saints, Fargo!" Snakeroot cried desperately as roaring, sawing flames were fanned even higher by a wind gust. "They can't hang on much longer, 'mano. The hell we gonna do?"

Fargo found no key. Before he could reply, however, gunfire blasted from in front of the prison. Fargo sprinted to the front corner of the burning building, shying back from the heat, just in time to see Snakeroot, standing boldly in the open, finish a shooting match with the remaining guard.

Fargo, intending to pitch in, hadn't even cleared leather before Snakeroot's last shot from the Remington penetrated the guard's lights and sent him collapsing to the ground.

"He was trying to sneak off, and I seen a key on his belt," Snakeroot explained as he ran toward the body. "So, like Skye Fargo, I took the bull by the horns."

As Snakeroot retrieved the double-bitted key, a shrill victory cry rose from the battlefield below them. The Apaches must have killed the last strangler. It would be a hollow victory, Fargo mused, if Hanchon and the rest perished.

Expecting the worst, the two choking men entered the smoke-billowing inferno and opened each cell with the passkey. All of the men were coughing hard, and a few had passed out from smoke inhalation, but the vents had helped spare them. Their comrades helped Fargo and Snakeroot carry them to safety.

Daniel Hanchon, however, was not among them. Even before Fargo could ask about him, a bald, middle-aged man with fire-smudged features approached him.

"Mr. Fargo? My name is Linton McCallister. I'm Reverend Hanchon's mining engineer. We were in the same cell."

" 'Were,' " Fargo repeated. "Did they kill him, Linton?"

"Worse, if you ask me. Hachita and Lutz came late last night and took him with them."

Fargo and Snakeroot exchanged a glance that spoke one word: *Amy*. Neither man would ever regret their labors today because a score of innocent men had been saved. But Hachita and Lutz were still above the ground, and the one man Fargo had been hired to save was not among these former prisoners. He never went back on his word, and this wasn't over.

"In hot weather," he told Snakeroot, "a fish always goes to the bottom. For Lutz that will be his house, with Hachita living in his pocket to protect him. We can end it or mend it, and this is way beyond mending. So we'll end it fast."

16

Fargo had eaten nothing but a hunk of jerky all day, so busy was he in helping to transport the former prisoners back to their homes and helping Eskiminzin patch up the Apache wounded. Three had also been killed, and Fargo cut three work mules out of the Lady Luck's corral to carry the dead home. Fargo had no doubt the mules would then furnish the funeral meat.

So famished was Fargo by sundown, not to mention exhausted and powder-blackened, that Amy's hot biscuits and pinto beans, flavored with dried onion, tasted like steak. Fargo finished his plate quickly and began cleaning his fingernails with a match. The three of them sat on the ground outside the jacal, plates in their laps. The fire had gone out, but one tallow candle burned on a flat stone, shaded from any trails above by thick clumps of mesquite.

"Sit still," Amy fussed at Snakeroot. She bathed his wound with a camphor-soaked cloth. "You got this trying to free my father, and I am eternally in your debt."

"In that case—"

"Quit while you're ahead," Fargo warned. "She's speaking figuratively. You're not in the Black Bear now, old son."

"*Vaya!* Go ask your mother for a dug. I earned my first kill today."

"Your second," Fargo corrected him. "One of your shots at the water hole wounded a strangler so bad that his buddies snuffed him out."

"Hell, why didn't you tell me?" Snakeroot protested. "Afraid of competition?"

"I knew you'd get all puffed up like you are now."

But Fargo grinned after he said this. He looked at Amy. "The lad's green, but solid wood. He stood tall in a walking showdown and won. Like I told you, your dad was hustled out last night, but thanks to Snakeroot getting that key in the nick of time, all the other men were saved."

Snakeroot was reveling in this rare praise. As soon as Amy had finished with his cheek, he was smoking his cheap, foul-smelling tobacco and waiting to hear more about his manly virtues.

"Then again," Fargo added, "they say even a blind hog will root up an acorn now and then. Maybe skinny just got lucky."

Snakeroot knew Fargo well enough by now not to take offense at the remark. He drank from a bottle of whiskey he'd filched from a dead vigilante, then lowered the bottle and wiped his lips on his sleeve.

"Cut the dust?" he asked Fargo, handing him the bottle.

"Skye," Amy said, "what's the point of Lutz's taking my father hostage?"

"Never mind his point. I think the man has only got one oar in the water. I also think he's out of useful plans now. But his mad will is set in stone, and he's not giving up. Besides, it's not completely insane to nab your father."

"Why not?"

"For one thing, he knows you value your father highly—enough to hire me, and risk your safety, to get him back. A hostage no one values will get him nowhere. Then again, he may not want a hostage."

Her delicate eyebrows arched. "I don't understand. Of course Father is a hos—oh! You mean . . . ?"

Fargo nodded. "It's possible he just intends to kill him—or already has. Lutz is obsessed with his plans for money and power, and he could see your father as the reason his empire is crumbling around him."

"One more argument why," Snakeroot chimed in, "if we don't finish this off quick, all we've done so far is wash bricks."

"Call this lad Sir Oracle," Fargo approved. "We can't wait. For now, anyway, most of Lutz's scurvy-ridden toughs are gone. But if we take the road of by-and-by, he'll have time to hire replacements and the bloodletting will begin."

"I saw a few stranglers escaping today," Snakeroot reminded him.

"Lutz might have a few plug-uglies left," Fargo said, "but unless he's paying them gambler's wages, I doubt it. That trash riding for him would kill their own mothers for a two-cent cigar. Hell, would you stick around after the turkey shoot at the water hole and this scrape today?"

"Yes, but will Hachita stick around?" Amy asked. "With Lutz, I mean?"

"I'd bet my horse he will. Hachita, unlike Lutz, knows it's over. But for one thing, he can't keep his eyes off Lupita, and he means to own her—you can see it in that pocked face of his. I'd say he also means to steal whatever he can from Lutz's house. And I know he wants a crack at killing me."

"All these hard cases need to be broomed, all right," Snakeroot spoke up. "But then comes law, Fargo, which is just government with a gun. That means I'll be jugged most of the time. Only white men can be drunk in the streets."

"If that's a whine aimed at me," Fargo replied, "tell me—how kind are Apaches to whites who sneak in among them and steal their property?"

"Hell, they fawn all over *you*, 'Son of Light.'"

"Both of you are being silly," Amy cut in. "How can you be so matter-of-fact in the midst of this tragedy? Back east, my father insists, some of those men who died today might have been saved by the county poorhouse. Out here, a desperate man has no choice except to turn to crime."

Fargo snorted. "County poorhouse, my sweet aunt. Most of these men committed serious crimes back east—that's why they're out here, ducking a summons."

"Well, Father is a preacher and sees it as a more complex problem."

"Fair enough," Fargo allowed.

"Yeah, but don't be surprised," Snakeroot said, "if your old man's views are different now." He left unspoken the thought: *If he's even alive.*

"Never mind Reverend Hanchon's views," Fargo said impatiently. "Snakeroot, you say there's a working cannon on the plaza?"

"On the north side. They say it was left by Coronado's men. Why?"

"You say it's a six-pounder," Fargo pressed. "Any shot for it?"

"Caleb Greene used to have some canister shot at his gun shop. One-ounce balls."

"That might work," Fargo said, eyes crimped in thought. "Might work fine."

"*Por dios*, a cannon? Aimed against Lutz's house?"

"Why not? I'd wager you don't know sic 'em about cannons. The damage can be controlled. Setting a fire to flush them out could set the whole town ablaze. And if we just rush them, I don't like Reverend Hanchon's chances."

"But, Skye," Amy said, "my father is probably in that house."

"Not in all of it, hon. If you take a hostage, aren't you going to keep him close to hand? That means the ground floor."

"Well . . ."

"Any way you slice it," Fargo reasoned, "we're going to have to take some risks. But we can pull this off. Lutz's type always over-rate themselves. The ability to make money isn't the same as the ability to survive out here."

A sudden, cool breeze rustled the mesquite pods all around them. Fargo sniffed the breeze, then stood up.

"Storm making up," he told the other two. "I doubt if we'll have any rain that makes it down to us, but there'll be strong wind and dry lightning. I hate to do it, but let's hobble the mounts, Snakeroot, case they get spooked."

"You know, Fargo," Snakeroot said as he rose from the ground, "I hate to say it, but you screwed the pooch today when you had a clear bead on Hachita and didn't shoot him."

"It's too dead to skin now," Fargo replied. "But, damn you, you're right. Unless he kills me first, I won't make that mistake again."

By ten p.m., howling, at times even tornadic, winds ripped through Tucson Valley and buffeted everything while ghostly tines of lightning shot down from the sky.

"My kind of weather," Bearcat Lutz told Hachita, watching the storm from a library window. "Just think, Fargo and his friends are going to get soaking wet."

"If Fargo is with them," Hachita begged to differ, "no one will get wet."

"All right, I know, he's a goddamn god, right? Where was the god at the water hole? Sitting on his ass, useless as tits on a boar hog. Ignore the legend and kill the man."

"Take the pinecone out of your ass," Hachita said in a gravel-pitted voice. His beloved Sharps was propped against his chair.

Using the rattan cane for support, Lutz turned around. "All right, I'll ease off. After all, it was a rough couple of days for the Committeemen."

"Especially for those who actually fought," the Hatchet reminded him bluntly.

Lutz ignored this. "You think they'll attack us tonight?"

"Fargo steps nowhere twice, so his actions can't be predicted. But I say no. Not so long as the preacher is alive—or they think he is."

Lutz, his face showing the strain of looming losses, began to pace. "I was a damn fool. God or no, we should have run Fargo off like a distempered wolf the moment he got here. Instead, I saw him as a source of diversion, a rube I could easily control."

"Control? *Vaya, hombre!* You cannot close-herd a man like Fargo."

"I see that, but *he's* the one who's wrong. He is one of these men who insist that things must forever remain as they are—especially the West. Hell, he's a relic doomed to grub like a savage. And *that's* what sells for a hero these days."

"Amy Hanchon bought it," Hachita said as he pushed out of his chair, "and I think Lupita did, too."

Hachita walked to the hallway door, shouting out to the two Committeemen who still worked for Bearcat. They were standing sentry at the front and back doors. Both men reported the all-secure. He returned to his chair.

"Bearcat, this is no time to talk of heroes and relics. Your brain is a strange one that worries about all the wrong things. We must decide about the preacher."

"What about him?"

"*Mira*, Crawley was right. Daniel Hanchon is dangerous if he is allowed to live. Why don't I go to his room right now and take care of it? No one need find out for days, and we can feed the body to Pablo Padilla's hogs. They even eat the clothing and bones."

"That might turn out to be the best plan," Lutz agreed. "But stay your hand a bit. Of course we're going to kill the sanctimonious bastard, but let's get our full use of him first. He might be a good bargaining chip."

Hachita scowled. "With Fargo out there, delay is not wise."

"Don't worry. The holy man will be going to glory soon enough. Speaking of him . . ."

Bearcat fished a gold watch from his fob pocket and thumbed back the cover. "Time to check on the prisoner."

He followed a wainscoted hallway smelling of beeswax, stopping at the last door on the right and unlocking it. Daniel Hanchon lay shackled to a narrow bed.

"Lutz," he pleaded, "you can only make it worse for yourself if you persist in this madness. Let me go, for the love of God."

Lutz walked slowly toward the bed. "God? Haven't you heard, Reverend? There's only one God west of the Mississippi, and his name is Sam Colt."

"As evil as you are, Lutz, I pray for your soul."

Outside, the wind howled and shook the house. Lutz stood next to the bed by now. "Don't presume on your white hairs, Hanchon. I've sent older men than you to their graves."

"That's common knowledge. And their blood will be on your hands come Judgment Day."

Lutz smacked the reverend so hard he left a bright red handprint on his face. "To hell with your weak-kneed religion, you pious old twat. How does your God feel about whores? Because right now Skye Fargo is playing hide-the-picket-pin with your daughter. All honeymoon and no wedding."

Hanchon, however, was pushed too hard by that slap. Not caring what his captor did, he turned his head and refused to speak.

"I'm sure you believe in miracles, holy man," Lutz said by way of parting. "Pray all you want, not even Fargo will save you. You started all this in motion and cost me a fortune. And I am personally going to kill you with my own hands, and it won't be quick."

Lutz didn't return to the library, but went on down the long central hallway to the master bedroom on the south side of the house. He found Lupita undressing behind a three-panel dressing screen, her wild tumble of coal black hair down for the night.

Lupita met his gaze and put a protective hand to her throat. "Bearcat, what is wrong? You look . . . different."

He laughed too loudly, almost shrilly. "Perhaps I just came to take what is a man's right."

"Yes, I can always tell you are a real man by the cathouse stink of your lilac hair tonic."

"You'd know about cathouse stink, all right."

Lupita studied his strange, almost messianic face and wisely bit back her retort, frightened by his manner and behavior.

He said, "You know I've decided to kill the preacher, eh?"

"What is that to me? You have murdered many people."

"Don't play dumb with me, you greaser bitch. It means there won't be a rape trial. Do you take my drift now?"

Lupita only nodded. Usually she gave Lutz the rough side of her tongue, but this was a different Lutz.

"That's right—I have no use for you now except what's between your legs, and all cats look alike in the dark. Anything you'd like to say *now* about Fargo's virility before a better man kills him?"

"I know nothing about his virility," she said submissively.

"You're a lying whore. Hachita says Fargo poked you. And I smelled that drifter all over you one night—the night you were too sore to do it with me. Right now the only reason you're alive is the fact that I promised you to Hachita if he performs well. So either I kill you or that ugly, pockmarked bastard gets to rut on you. *Chica*, looks like you're caught between a sawmill and a shootout. Hell, I'd even say your only hope is Skye Fargo."

17

The nighttime storm hardly affected the three people sleeping in the crude brush hut east of Tucson. There was only a spitting of rain, and the raging winds were softened by the depth of the canyon.

Nonetheless, Fargo was up well before sunrise, unable to sleep. He checked on the mounts and loosened their hobbles. Then he quietly built up a small fire against the sharp chill, setting last night's coffee in the flames to heat up.

He gauged the time by judging the height of the dawn star in the east. When it was time, he woke Amy and Snakeroot.

"*Hijo*, this ground is hard," Snakeroot complained, rubbing the small of his back as he came out of the hut. "I thought sand was soft?"

"It is," Fargo told him, "unless you spread your blankets over a buried rock."

Snakeroot ducked into the hut and came out fuming. Amy made peals of mirth behind him.

"Fargo, you ornery bastard, you *knew* I was on a rock and never even told me."

"Tenderfoot, a man that stupid deserves to suffer. Maybe you'll look closer next time you sleep on the ground."

Snakeroot frowned, began to look foolish, then finally burst out laughing. "Ain't *I* the Dan'l Boone?"

The sun appeared as a salmon pink streak on the horizon. Some of the flowering cacti were in bloom, and Fargo's finely honed sense of smell detected their delicate, perfumed scent. Far away, a coyote ended his nighttime prowling with a long, wavering howl that trailed off into yipping barks.

Amy finally emerged, her face puffy with worry and lack of sleep.

"Skye," she said right off as if she'd rehearsed it, "every step

138

you've taken in this battle, all I did was fret and worry. Secretly, I didn't think you could survive this long. So now I'm going to take your attitude—that we *can* win this."

"Sure we can," Snakeroot said, "but why do we have to do it from here instead of Tucson? Hell, we've erased most of Bearcat's army."

Fargo shook his head. "What are you jabbering about? I already told you we can't let Amy near that town until this things is played through. Lutz and Hachita are still around. And do *you* want to leave her out here alone?"

Snakeroot knew Fargo was right, but his mood was too surly to acknowledge it. The two men cleaned and loaded their weapons while Amy made pan bread.

"You still got that wild hare of an idea about the cannon?" Snakeroot asked.

"It's no wild hare," Fargo gainsaid. "If that cannon hasn't been spiked, and it hasn't cracked over time, it'll likely work. You got a better idea?"

"Nope. *No tengo nada.*"

"That's what I figured. Pups like to bark like full-grown dogs."

Amy clasped her hands. "Skye, don't forget my father is probably inside that house."

"All my plans revolve around that assumption, lady. And *you* don't forget I'll have to take risks."

With the sun dull red and big in the east, the two men tacked their mounts and rode due west into Tucson.

"Let's keep our mounts close," Fargo said as they trotted through the narrow cultivation belt that encircled Tucson. "Lutz is desperate now, openly my enemy, and it would be easy to have them killed at a livery."

"Hell, this mule could be replaced easy," Snakeroot remarked. "But your Ovaro has no peer."

"My sentiments exactly."

Instead of the grim scene Fargo expected, however, Tucson seemed to be in a festive mood—except for the Sagebrush Saloon, whose entrance was boarded over. The crowd at the Black Bear had spilled out onto the plaza, the early hour be damned. A few of them cheered when they spotted Fargo and Snakeroot.

"Hep! Hep!" shouted a teamster who'd made it through the desert, cracking his long whip and guiding his overloaded freight wagon around a drunk who lay sprawled on the plaza.

"Just like the good old days," Snakeroot said, "when a man could fall asleep on the plaza and not wake up in Lutz's mine. One of his thugs started to take me once, but when he was able to pick me up off the ground with one hand, he tossed me back."

They rode a few steps farther, and Snakeroot spoke up again.

"Can you read that, Fargo?" he asked, pointing to a broadside just then being plastered to a wall. "I never went to school."

"Teach yourself," Fargo said. "That's what I did. Hang on."

Fargo tugged rein to wheel the Ovaro around, riding closer to the sign. "It's a notice about a meeting tonight to form the Citizens' Guard to replace the crooked bunch. It calls for honest, employed men to enforce the laws until real law arrives."

"Some of these men talking on the plaza were in that prison bunch," Snakeroot marveled, looking around. "They ain't wasting no time licking their wounds."

"Good for them," Fargo said. "They best do it right, though, because I suspect it's going to be a long time before they get real starpackers out here."

Fargo couldn't be sure, as they edged closer to Lutz's house, that this crowd didn't hide killers notching their sights on him. He loosened the Henry in its boot and knocked back the Colt's riding thong.

"Best not ride too close," Fargo said, reining in when he'd reached the boarded-up dance hall. Lutz's house was visible from here.

"I wouldn't advise it, either," Snakeroot said. "I hear the Hatchet ain't so hot with a handgun, but with his Sharps he'll pick us off like lice from a blanket. And he does his best work with the hatchet. Hacking away close up, or burying the hatchet up to its helve at seventy-five feet."

"Mr. Fargo!"

A man riding a light tan palomino with an ivory mane and tail spurred toward Fargo and Snakeroot. Fargo recognized Linton McCallister, who had shared a cell with Reverend Hanchon.

"Looks like you boys are pitching into the game," Fargo greeted him.

"It's belated, but we're doing what we can, Mr. Fargo. Right now five men are headed out to the Lady Luck. They're going to shove all the dead bodies into an old shaft and cover it. We mean to seize that mine as compensation for false imprisonment and slave labor."

"That's the gait," Fargo approved. "I see you're moving fast here in town, too."

McCallister nodded. "Men will be posted out here all the time, starting this morning. But so long as Daniel may be in that house, Lutz has got the whip hand. Especially with Hachita in there."

"You sure he is?" Fargo asked.

McCallister nodded. "Right before you got here, he went to Benny Fong's café and came out with a lot of food on a tray. None of us had the backbone to brace him."

"Wise choice," Fargo said. "But we'll get him."

"Maybe we can just starve them out," Snakeroot suggested. "The Hatchet wouldn't pull that strolling-to-the-café crap if you're standing out front of it."

"Prob'ly take too long," Fargo decided. "And when Bearcat finally snaps to the fact that it's curtains for him, why not kill his worst enemy, Reverend Hanchon, first? I don't favor any plan that drags this out. You take the fight to your enemy hard and fast."

"Makes sense," McCallister agreed. "Just like you broke that heavy door apart yesterday. But how?"

Fargo pointed to the battered black cannon on the north side of the plaza, spattered by bird droppings. "That, if it works. Lutz has a strong stomach when it comes to ordering murders, but I think he's a coward. Right now he's nerve-jangled, and knocking the house down around him just might make him crater."

"He still might kill the reverend," Snakeroot said. "Yesterday you said Lutz will never crater, that he'll have to be killed."

"In the Bearcat's case, one's the same as the other."

"Seems to me," Linton McCallister put in, "Daniel's life is at risk no matter what we do. Lutz is expecting something humdrum like a massed attack or a fire. He's not looking for a cannon, and neither is Hachita."

"And of the two," Fargo mused alloud, "Hachita is the greater threat."

Fargo's hat spun off, and an eyeblink later the sound of the big-bore Sharps sounded like a cannon itself.

"Wheel!" Fargo barked, and all three men moved down the plaza until Hachita had no angle on them.

Fargo felt his scalp sweat when he realized how close that shot was—and from a nearly impossible angle. Fargo lassoed his hat and pulled it back to him.

"Boys," he told the other two, "that tears it for me. I want those two cold, and I want it damn quick. Snakeroot, you see about lead shot at the gun store. We still need powder, too."

"Shit! We just ruined several kegs two nights ago."

"You're in luck for black powder," McCallister said. "Daniel's warehouse is on Manzano Street, and we can spare some."

Snakeroot and McCallister rode off in different directions. Fargo noticed a group of men standing nearby, as if awaiting orders.

"Say, boys," Fargo called out. "Unless you're friends of Bearcat Lutz, I could sure use help muscling that old cannon about a hundred feet or so. Anybody for a hernia?"

"We'll do it if you promise to blow it right up Lutz's ass!" shouted a thin, whip-scarred man Fargo recognized as one of the prisoners. "And that unholy bastard Hachita with him."

Fargo didn't blame them for their murderous rage. "Vengeance is mine" and "turn the other cheek" were useful ideas, at times, but only went so far when men were being flogged to death and deprived of water in the hot sun.

"We'll also need some volunteers to form a bucket brigade," he said. "With the town so dry, we could spark a fire somehow."

"I'll take charge of that," said the whip-scarred former prisoner.

"We'll put a ribbon on it, boys, and soon," Fargo promised. "Follow me, but keep your heads tucked and try to stay sideways to the house—makes less target. Whatever you do, don't drift in any closer to Lutz's house than you have to. Hachita could be notching his sights on us."

Crossing the plaza from south to north, swinging wide of the house, Fargo led the way toward the old Spanish cannon. McCallister returned in jig time with the powder in a tight wooden keg. He was in time to join a dozen other men who took up positions behind the gun carriage. Fargo took the most dangerous spot, supporting the tip of the muzzle.

"Careful!" he warned again. "We only need to wheel it about a hundred feet closer to the house to ensure well-placed shots. But before we fire it, I have to give Lutz and the Hatchet a chance to surrender. I'd like to avoid putting the reverend at risk."

Snakeroot rode up. "All Caleb has are one-ounce balls. He said you can ram in ninety-six of them tight and it will seal the bore like a six-pound ball. I got all he had, and when he found out what it was for, there was no charge."

He swung down and handed Fargo a heavy pail of lead shot. Fargo set it aside. "That's a little dicey in an old piece like this, but we'll have to chance it."

McCallister counted out the lead balls while another man found a pole and rags for ramming the load. Fargo's long arm reached into the muzzle as far as he could and pulled some leaves and two whiskey bottles out of it. He poured the powder into the firing chamber, rammed it home tight, then poured balls down the smooth bore and rammed them tight.

"Let's go boys!" he shouted. "Snakeroot, get on that carriage. *Heave!*"

By sheer dint of will and muscle they dragged the heavy cannon farther out onto the plaza, about fifty yards in front of Lutz's house. The Big Fifty spoke from a window, and a man who had carelessly exposed too much of his body went down gushing blood from a direct hit to the heart.

"Everybody clear out!" Fargo snapped. "You, too, Snakeroot, this job calls for a one-man outfit. Some of you fellows take the body. Quick, before the Hatchet reloads."

Everyone else had retreated, and Fargo was ducking behind the gun carriage, when the next shot ricocheted off the cannon, throwing sparks.

"Hey, Fargo!" Hachita's voice roared out. "That one damn near took your pizzle off! Maybe this next one will geld you, *verdad*?"

Fargo ignored the taunt, and spoke directly to the man giving the orders. "Lutz!" he bellowed. "Use your head! You can give up now or make us come in. And we don't come in until that house is scrap wood around your ears."

Lutz's voice was shrill and strained. "Kiss my ass, Fargo, you Indian lover! That old piece doesn't work, you're just running a bluff. Hell, it hasn't been fired since the conquistadors."

"If I was you and Hachita, I wouldn't want to find out if it's a bluff."

"It's a bluff," Lutz insisted. "Hanchon is here, and you won't risk killing him."

Again Hachita fired his Big Fifty, this time aiming under the carriage, and Fargo felt a sharp tug as the slug ripped through his left trousers leg. Each shot was homing in closer, and even a wound from that Big Fifty could easily shock a man to death.

"You must have grabbed Hanchon for a reason," Fargo said. "Whatever you think he's worth, let's dicker. What do you want?"

"My terms are reasonable. I want a legally drawn grant of immunity against any supposed crimes, signed by every man whom I imprisoned. That immunity must include Hachita."

"Or he'll kill you, right?"

"Curb your mouth or the deal's off. I also want safe passage out of here for the two of us. I keep Reverend Hanchon until we're safe, then turn him loose."

Fargo gave a harsh bark of laughter. "You insane son of a bitch, do you really think you can shit all over these men and then just waltz on out of here like it's none of your business? You want to bring down the thunder, do you? Well, by the Lord Harry, here she comes!"

Fargo made one final check of the gun's angle, thumb-scratched a lucifer into flame, then shook it out as an idea occurred to him.

"Snakeroot!"

"Yo!"

"The reverend and Lupita are in there, and likely some servants. It's best if they're covered down tight before I fire up this barn leveler. On my command, you, Linton, and the rest start pouring lead into the house. Shoot the windows, but aim high on the glass to avoid killing. You—"

The Big Fifty cracked just after the slug punched into the adobe bricks, flecks of it stinging a kneeling Fargo like a swarm of bees. Hachita had figured out how to aim under the gun, and he was getting frighteningly accurate.

Fargo waited until the men—he counted eight—had taken up a skirmish line.

"Don't stop firing," he told them, "until you hear this six-pounder go off."

Fargo had overheard several skeptics insist the retired cannon wouldn't fire, it would simply explode, a victim of age and old-fashioned casting techniques. He allowed for that, but knew these old cannons were solid work.

He took out another match. "Let 'er rip, boys!" he shouted to his informal militia. Rifles and handguns opened up, and before long every front window of Lutz's house was shattered. Bullets riddled the door and tattooed the wood facade of the house.

Fargo lit the match and held it to the touchhole, fully aware the base of the cannon could blow wide apart and send him to the Happy Hunting Grounds. The powder caught instantly, a massive explosion rocking the gun back, and several feet of flames whooshed from the muzzle.

Fargo had aimed at the front left turret. At this distance there was little time for the shot pattern to spread, and with near precision, the giant fist of lead smashed the turret to kindling. The riflemen ceased fire, jaws dropping, at the spectacle of broken boards raining down onto the plaza.

In the shocked, ensuing silence, Fargo heard a piercing female scream. But it was one of abject fear, not pain.

"Hijo!" Snakeroot said. "That old whore can still kick."

"It survived," Fargo said in a low tone. "But a hairline crack opened up just above the touchhole."

The Sharps spoke, and a chunk of dried wood spun away from the gun carriage.

"Keep it up, Fargo!" Lutz's clearly shaken voice said. "One more bonehead play like that, and the reverend delivers his next sermon from a cloud."

Fargo didn't like it. He felt Lutz might be bluffing, that he had no stomach for another blast from hell's mouth. The only way to find out was to call his bluff.

"The reverend ain't all that matters," Fargo shouted back. "Since you thumb your nose at surrender, the men out here have told me to kill you—you, and the Hatchet. Sentence has been passed."

"Don't play master stallion with me, Fargo. You know my demands. Blast my house one more time, and you'll have to bury Hanchon with a rake."

More gaudy patter, Fargo hoped. He ignored it, busy counting out six pounds' worth of lead balls. He rammed home powder and loads, timing his movements between shots from Hachita's Big Fifty.

And, all the time, worried about that hairline crack. Would the next explosion rip open a wide seam, flames incinerating him? He had to carry out the threat, or this standoff would never be over.

Fargo touched a match to the hole, averting his face, and felt the powder seem to suck it down. The blast this time rocked the cannon back several feet and widened the crack, but the cast iron held. The right front turret of Lutz's house, however, did not. It shattered into wood chips, exposing upstairs rooms.

"Lower your hammers!" Lutz shouted, desperation spiking his voice. "Fargo, I have an offer for you. Don't shoot when I come outside. Hachita is with the reverend, and he won't need much excuse to kill him."

18

Every man on the square stood rooted, watching the drama unfold. Lutz's front door opened, but he stopped only two paces onto the veranda.

Fargo couldn't credit his own eyes. With his house literally crumbling down around him, Lutz wore a black-and-white-striped smoking jacket with velvet lapels.

"No lo creo," Snakeroot muttered. "I don't believe it. The bastard's gone loco. For him, everything hangs by a thread, and he should be scared pukey. But he's still the rich man of leisure."

"I'm unarmed, Fargo," Lutz shouted. "No hideout guns, either. Come over closer so we can discuss terms."

"Eat shit, *pendejo*!" Snakeroot shouted. "You think Fargo is stupid enough to make it easy for Hachita?"

"Pack it in, kid," Fargo snapped. "I'm the topkick right now. Bearcat, I can hear you fine from where you are, and the rest have a right to hear it, too."

"The rest can kiss my ass! This town was a tent city when I arrived here. Hell, men were shitting where they ate and drinking cholera water. I turned all that around."

"Yeah," Fargo said, "you're a regular damn founding father, all right. Look, pare the cheese closer to the rind—name your terms."

"You know the deal I suggested just before you illegally fired on my house? The immunity deal?"

"Get over your pipe dream, poncy man, and look at the hard-cash facts. I told you that's off the table. That's the will of the citizens, too."

"But what if," Lutz wheedled, "we add an element? Such as, you and Hachita will settle the issue in personal combat. No guns because Hachita admits he's no draw-shoot artist. You'll each have a hatchet."

Snakeroot violently shook his head no.

"Rather use my knife," Fargo said without hesitation. Lutz turned to confer with someone in the house, presumably Hachita.

"By the Virgin, Fargo, don't you believe me?" Snakeroot demanded. "Up near the Republican River, Hachita once defeated six armed Sioux warriors with only his hatchet."

"I don't care if he skinned out fifty Texas Rangers and a herd of charging elephants. What a man supposedly did in the past doesn't matter. I watched that ruthless bastard beat a helpless old man to death. This is a brand-new day, and I aim to gut that son of a bitch."

"Fargo, your terms are fine," Lutz called over. "If I win, I get my earlier deal. If you win, the reverend goes free and I surrender. No admission of guilt, mind you."

"Boys," Fargo said quietly to the nearby men, "I told Lutz those were *my* terms—I never said the new Citizens' Guard approved. We're making the medicine, and Lutz is taking it. If Hachita sends me under, you owe nothing to Bearcat."

"Oh, we owe him plenty," Linton McCallister said. "I plan to make a tobacco pouch out of his scrotum."

"All right so far, Bearcat!" Fargo replied. "Where do we fight?"

"How 'bout halfway between where you and I are standing?"

"That's all right. Tell Hachita to leave any firearms in the house. I'll ground mine."

"Fargo," Snakeroot said urgently, "Hachita likes to sneak-throw that hatchet as he closes for the fight."

Fargo unbuckled his gun belt. "That's all right if you score a hit, but leaves you without a weapon if you don't. He'll hang on to it."

"If he pulls a hideout gun on you," Snakeroot said, "we'll drill him full of holes."

"Like hell you will. I'm in the line of fire. All you boys just keep your muzzles lowered. It'll be a hell-buster, but that old boy is crossing over."

Fargo tugged the Arkansas Toothpick from his boot, feeling the perfect balance of the long, strong blade. He watched Hachita, wearing the familiar bleached canvas trousers, emerge from the house holding his double-bladed throwing hachet.

Fargo stopped at the halfway point and waited for his opponent. Hachita's eyes were hard, flat chips of flint. He stopped about six feet away from Fargo. "Time to call in the cards, Trailsman."

"Do-si-do and don't let go," Fargo sang like a square-dance caller, adding a wink that affected Hachita like a sharp spur.

"Bridge the gap, *cabrón*," he growled, slicing the air with his hatchet as he circled his opponent. The weapon was double dangerous because it could slice deep from two directions. Fargo could almost whiff his rage.

"I know how this works," Fargo said calmly. "You dazzle me with your fancy circus act while you close in close enough to kill me. So I think I'll do *this*."

Hachita had forgotten about Fargo's long reach. He thrust his Arkansas Toothpick out fast as a rattler striking, sinking an inch or so of steel into Hachita's left thigh. The Mexican howled and scooted backward.

Quick as eyesight, however, Hachita burst forward and took a deadly swipe at Fargo's torso. The Trailsman, well balanced on the balls of his feet, was able to leap backward in time to avoid a lethal wound. The razor-sharp blade tore open his shirt and burned a long, shallow cut across his skin.

"*Gut* the son of a bitch, Hachita!" Lutz urged from the veranda. "Watch those long arms."

A heart-skip later, Hachita's hobnailed boot slammed into Fargo's gut like a mule kick. Fargo reeled backward, arms windmilling the air. Hachita immediately followed this move with a lunge, his deadly weapon slicing so close to vitals that Fargo could feel the wind from it.

"The great legend," Hachita mocked. "Look at him! Still hiding his fear behind that—*annh*!"

Fargo stopped the lunge by puncturing Hachita's other thigh, deeper this time. Blood seeped steadily from two wounds, and Hachita looked less brash.

Both men circled warily, and Fargo squared his shoulders. "I been keeping accounts, and you owe plenty. A debt you inherited from Crawley. And you're going to pay it off just like he did."

"Wrong, you crusading bastard. They say a fish always looks bigger underwater, just like a man looks bigger in legend. Up close, Fargo, you are just another trail bum."

"And yet the woman you lust for prefers me," Fargo taunted. "Any woman would mate with a coyote over you. Fewer fleas."

Rage worked Hachita's face into a twisted mask of hate, the

emotion Fargo always preferred in his opponents. It destroyed the cool head needed to win.

"Let's see your famous moves, Hachita. I'm bored with listening to your mouth. You're hiding your fear behind brave words. If you've got a set on you, kill me now."

The goading worked. Hachita began a savage assault, driving in at Fargo while his hatchet seemed a blur of speed, slashing dangerously close. When the moment was just right, Fargo threw up a left-arm block while his right drove his knife deep and low into Hachita's guts. Fargo drove through, not at, ripping apart intestines and releasing a sudden puff of body heat. At the last moment Fargo gave his blade the "Spanish twist" to tear the vitals open even more.

This time the pain was so horrible that Hachita only sucked in a hissing breath. The solid man hit the plaza like a sack of salt, his blood rapidly forming a large, spreading puddle.

"Jesus, Fargo," he managed, coughing up gobs of blood, "you've killed me."

"What'd you expect, a sugar tit? You started this, Hachita, I only finished it. Burn in hell, you murdering bastard."

Fargo rose and turned to Bearcat, whose face had turned green as old brass while he watched his only protector bleed out like a stuck hog. Fargo took one step in his direction, and the coward bolted toward the house.

Fargo dove to the ground. "Shoot him, boys, before he gets to the rev!"

Several weapons opened up, but like most cowards, Lutz was lightning fast at saving his own worthless hide. He made it back inside even as bullets chewed at the door.

"Stop gawking like a ninny," Fargo snapped at Snakeroot, who stared in morbid fascination as Hachita began his death rattle. "You and Linton come with me. Let's go in there now and stop that son of a bitch."

Fargo had to worry about any remaining stranglers at Lutz's house. Instead of trying to flush them out, leaving Hanchon and probably Lupita at risk, Fargo decided to storm the house.

To his uneasy surprise, the front door was unlocked. He burst in, the rest following him. The damage to the front turrets had also knocked down paintings and left plaster dust in the heart of the house.

"Every man fan out," he ordered. "We'll start with this floor and work up."

Before anyone could move, however, a loud gunshot very nearby sent ice into Fargo's veins.

"There goes the reverend," Snakeroot said. "Damn, we got so close. Now we have to tell Amy."

Fargo ignored him, cat-footing toward the open library door. He peered cautiously inside. "Well, God kiss me."

The other two crowded up behind him and stared inside.

"So it's finally happened," Linton said. "Rot in hell, you venal scum."

Bearcat Lutz had slumped dead onto his desk, a good chunk of his head sprayed all over the wall behind him. The big weapon he'd used to do it was still clutched in his right hand.

"That's a Colt Dragoon," Fargo said. "I've dropped a buffalo with one. Bearcat wanted to be sure he got the job done. And once the kingpin is knocked over, any paid killers have scattered."

"Who is that?" a faint voice called from down the hall. "What's going on?"

"That's Daniel," Linton exclaimed, hurrying out of the library. Fargo and Snakeroot hung back a few moments, looking at the cowardly, demented man who had caused so much suffering in Tucson.

"He's just rotting meat now," Snakeroot said. "But for a time, *caramba*! He turned hell inside out around here."

"It's not over with him," Fargo warned. "This is a mining center, and you folks will need to head the trouble off fast. Unless all you want left are orphans and bachelors. And ride herd on these criminal gangs that are forming out here, on the model of the Border Ruffians back in Missouri and Kansas."

"Reverend Hanchon's fine!" Linton's voice called out. "A cut lip and some bruises, but fine."

Fargo and Snakeroot sent each other a grin and headed down the hallway to see him.

"Tell me, runt," Fargo asked Snakeroot, "still worried about telling Amy?"

19

Fargo relaxed in the chair as a smiling barber slapped bay rum tonic on his fresh-shaven face.

"There you go, Mr. Fargo," the barber said. "Bath, haircut, shave. Four bits."

Fargo flipped him a silver dollar. He had just collected good wages from Reverend Hanchon and was in a generous mood. "Keep the change."

"'Preciate it. Hope to see you back in Tucson soon."

Fargo stopped with his hand on the doorknob, watching the bustling crowd on the plaza. Only two days since Bearcat Lutz blew his brains out, and already Tucson felt like a city rejuvenated. How, he wondered, could such a weak and cowardly man have controlled this city like a hand puppet?

"Actually," he replied to the barber, "I plan to fight shy of all towns for a spell. But I'll ride back here eventually. I like the lay of the land."

Watching Bearcat Lutz, and listening to his ambition and greed, had taught Fargo a bleak lesson: The Trailsman didn't like it one whit, but he knew the days of saddles and spurs and open range would soon enough give way to trains and cities, to smoke and filth and stink and the dough-bellied men who would die without stores. And no place was safe. With his own eyes Fargo had seen a sawmill operating in the Canadian Rockies.

He strolled back along the plaza to the Hanchons' place, gratified to see that the Sagebrush was still tightly boarded. When he arrived, Daniel and Amy Hanchon, and Snakeroot, were waiting for him in front of the house.

"Must you leave so soon, Mr. Fargo?" the reverend asked. "I'll bet we could salvage that job with Butterfield."

"Thanks, Reverend, but my needle's pointing west. I hear the Mormons out in San Bernardino need mail riders."

"Well, each man to his destiny. I suppose this place will still be a heller, Mr. Fargo. But thanks to you, it won't be a literal hell."

Fargo nodded toward Snakeroot. "Don't forget the skinny runt here. I guessed right the first time I saw him—he *has* got Apache blood and courage. Matter fact, it was Snakeroot alone who got all you men out of the burning prison in time. He stood up in a gun battle to get that key."

"Oh, nobody's forgetting *that*," Amy assured him, putting an arm over the mixed-breed's skinny shoulders. "The new town council has already given him a house on the plaza, so he won't be sleeping in a hog's-head."

"I liked it," Snakeroot protested weakly. "No floors to sweep."

"The Citizens' Guard is enforcing the law," Hanchon said, "but will stand down when real law arrives. All property seized by Lutz's Committee is being returned to the rightful owners."

"The one's that are still alive," Amy interjected.

"As for the Lady Luck," the reverend said, whip scars marring his cheeks, "it's going to be auctioned off among the rich mine owners around the world. Some of the proceeds will go to the widows of the men Lutz killed."

"How about you two?" Fargo asked, looking from the reverend to his daughter.

"Dad's staying," Amy said proudly. "And he plans to run for Territorial Governor. But I'm going back to Illinois. I've seen too much death and violence, and I'm tired of sleeping with a weapon."

Fargo flashed his strong white teeth. "Good, I'm glad to hear it. We'll be losing a beautiful woman, but this is still too far west for females."

Snakeroot had been uncharacteristically quiet. Now, as Fargo prepared to stop by the livery for his horse, Snakeroot spoke up awkwardly.

"Fargo? You know, when you first got here . . . I mean, when . . ."

"Crack the nut and expose the meat," Fargo snapped, winking at the others.

"*Hijo!* You are a hard man, Fargo, but I like you."

"I like you, too, but that doesn't mean we're swapping spit."

Fargo waved to everyone and turned to leave.

"Momentito!" Snakeroot called behind him. "Just a second, you forgot your Remington."

"Keep it, *bravo*. You sure's hell earned it. And what did I tell you about shooting?"

"Never fire," Snakeroot answered promptly, "until I am assured of a hit."

"Remember that, old son, and remember this: Skye Fargo is mighty damn proud to have known you. Without you I would have been killed."

Snakeroot looked stunned. "Hell, Fargo, I didn't—"

"Kid?"

"Yeah?"

"Go wipe your damn nose."

Both men grinning wide, Fargo walked away.

Fargo paid for the Ovaro's last feed and rubdown in Tucson, feeling not at all guilty that he was still spending Lutz's silver pesos instead of the gold quarter-eagles Hanchon had paid him. At least it was going to good use now instead of paying murderers.

As he led the Ovaro across the hoof-packed yard to tack him and switch the tapaderos for his usual stirrups, he decided to ride past Lutz's seriously damaged house one last time. He was gazing at the shattered south turret when he heard a familiar summons.

"Psst! Fargo, over here."

Astounded, he shifted his gaze to the master bedroom window. Lupita hung out of it, wearing a white dress that lifted her breasts into view with daring candor. Like a moth to a flame, Fargo rode in closer.

"Cupcake, what are you doing here?" Fargo demanded. "Hell, behind you I can see a collapsed wall."

"I have lived in worse. As for why am I here, our good citizens," she said, sarcasm edging her voice, "stole almost everything in the house. But I moved quickly and found the places where Bearcat hid money. I do not have to work for months, perhaps years, and why not stay here? You see, the place has a very good bed, *verdad*? And good beds are rare in Tucson."

"Very true."

"Does Amy Hanchon have a good bed, Fargo?"

"I don't recall."

Her laughter climbed the scale like a musical instrument. "You remember every bed you've . . . slept in. Tell me, Fargo—who is better? Me or Amy Hanchon? She of the pasty face?"

"You're trying to haze me into thorns," Fargo protested. "It's like riding two excellent horses—all you can say is they're both excellent."

"Do you know something?" she said. "I would never have testified against Reverend Hanchon. Read this."

She handed him a neatly printed letter. In it, she asserted that Lutz forced her, under threat of death, to accuse Hanchon of rape.

"I had this ready," she explained. "But Bearcat made it easy for all of us. His miner's court died with him."

"Bearcat was just a bad dream, hon."

"But you are a good one—my randy stallion. Do you know how many times, since we made love, that I have touched myself to quench the fire?"

Fargo swallowed hard. "That's no fair, talking like that. Gets a man all het up."

"Is this unfair?" She unhooked her dress and let the top part fall to her waist, baring those caramel-colored globes with the chocolate nipples. "*Must* you leave right now?"

Fargo shifted in his saddle. "Hell, I don't want to be impolite, do I? I'll go put my stallion out back in the stable."

"Good!" she called after him. "And when you come back, I will ride *my* stallion until he bucks me off."

LOOKING FORWARD!
The following is the opening section of the next novel in the exciting *Trailsman* series from Signet:

THE TRAILSMAN #331
NORTHWOODS NIGHTMARE

The spectacular wilds of British Columbia, 1861—
where the trails were few but the ways to die were many.

Skye Fargo saw the black bear before it saw him.

A big man, broad of shoulder and narrow at the hips, he sat tall in the saddle. He spotted the bear when it came out of the thick woods onto the trail, and stopped.

Fargo quickly drew rein. He wasn't too concerned. He had a Colt strapped around his waist, over his buckskins. In a sheath in his boot nestled a razor-edged Arkansas toothpick. The splash of white and black under him was an Ovaro. Fargo had been riding the stallion for years now and would go on riding it until it died or he did. He'd never had a horse so dependable.

Fargo waited for the bear to move on. That it was a black bear and not a griz was in his favor. Black bears rarely attacked people. This one was big, though, as big as any he ever came across. But then, the bears were like everything else in the colony of British Columbia.

Fargo didn't know what it was: the land, the water, the soil, the fact there were so few people, but the wildlife and the plant life all seemed to be bigger north of the border.

An old-timer once told Fargo that was the way it had been in the States back in the old days. Where humans were few, the animals grew, and grew. Then waves of emigrants, pushing west, killed off the big ones, and the game that came along after that never got the chance to grow as big as those before. They were killed off to fill supper pots and so their pelts could be made into clothes and rugs.

Fargo liked that part about few humans. He was fond of the quiet places, the lonely places, the places hardly any whites ever saw. It was why folks called him the Trailsman. It was why the army relied on him so often as a scout. It was why others hired him as a guide.

That was what Fargo was doing at the moment, guiding. A quarter of a mile back down the trail came his party. He'd gone on ahead to check the trail and keep an eye out for game, and now this black bear had come along and brought him to a stop.

It was late afternoon and Fargo had spent all day in the saddle. He could use a cup of coffee and a hot meal. Stretching, he idly gazed at pillowy clouds floating through the blue British Columbia sky. Then he glanced up the trail, and gave a start.

The black bear was coming toward him.

Fargo dropped his hand to his Colt. He'd rather avoid the bear than shoot it. Bears took a lot more butchering than deer, and some people weren't as fond of bear meat as they were of venison. Personally, he liked bear meat just fine, but some of those in the party he was guiding struck him as finicky.

The bear was still coming.

Fargo rose in the stirrups and hollered, "Skedaddle, you idiot." Black bears were skittish. They often ran at the sound of a human voice. But not this one. It raised its nose and sniffed a few times and then kept on lumbering toward him.

"Hell." Fargo reined around and tapped his spurs. He would go back down the trail. The bear would realize he wasn't a threat and go its merry way. He went around a bend and glanced back.

The bear came trotting after him.

"Son of a bitch." Fargo scowled. The bear was moving fast, not a full-out lope, but fast. Clearly, it had decided that he or the Ovaro was worth catching. And what a bear could catch, it ate.

Fargo used his spurs again, bringing the stallion to a trot. He trotted around the next bend and went fifty more yards besides, and again drew rein. Surely, he told himself, the black bear had given up.

Here it came, lumbering after him.

"Damn contrary critter." Fargo was mad. He was trying his best to spare the thing and it wanted him for its dinner. Once more he wheeled and this time he rode a good distance at a full gallop, enough to show the bear it had no chance of catching him. Bears were as fast as horses over short spurts, but a horse with a big enough lead usually left a bear eating its dust.

Fargo came to a stop and reined broadside to the trail. He figured that was the end of it. He figured the bear had given up and gone off into the forest in search of easier prey. He waited to be proven right—and was proven wrong.

Once more the black bear appeared, and when it saw him, it ran faster.

Enough was enough. The day Fargo couldn't outsmart a bear was the day he hung up his Colt, found himself a rocking chair somewhere, and put himself out to pasture. He galloped to the next turn and on around. Once out of the bear's sight, he reined into the trees. The undergrowth was so thick, it only took him a few moments to find cover where he could see the trail without being seen.

The seconds went by and Fargo began to think that this time the bear had gotten it through its thick head that it couldn't catch him, when there it was, its heavy paws thudding the ground, breathing like a bellows. It ran past his hiding place and soon was out of sight around the next bend.

Chuckling, Fargo gigged the Ovaro and turned up the trail to continue on his way. With the bear behind him he had nothing to worry about. But then it hit him. The bear was now between him and those he was guiding—*and heading right toward them.*

Fargo wheeled the Ovaro. The odds of the bear attacking a party as large as his was small, but this bear wasn't acting as a bear should. He spurred to a trot, confident he would soon catch up.

Minutes went by, and there was no sign of the bear. Fargo grew surer and surer the bear had given up and gone off into the forest. He was congratulating himself on outsmarting it when the first shot cracked, and then another. There was a roar, and someone screamed.

The bear was attacking them.

Blistering the air with fiery oaths, Fargo sped to their aid. From the shrieks and the cries at least one person was down and there might be more. Most were city dwellers, and prone to panic at a time like this, and too often panic led to dead.

Fargo reached down and shucked his Henry rifle from the saddle scabbard. The brass receiver gleamed as he levered a round into the chamber. The bear was as good as dead. It just didn't know it yet.

Another scream knifed the air. The bear must be wreaking havoc. Then a rifle boomed like a cannon.

McKern's Sharps, Fargo reckoned, and he smiled. A heavy-caliber Sharps could drop most anything in its tracks. No doubt the bear was dead.

A roar proved him wrong.

That might mean McKern was down, too. Fargo hoped not. The old man was one of the two people in that bunch he counted on.

Fargo swept around a bend and then around another and came on a scene straight from every guide's worst nightmare.

The bear must have torn into them before they realized it was there. Three horses were down, whinnying and thrashing and kicking, one with blood spurting from a clawed throat. Their riders were down, too, and two weren't moving. The third was McKern. The old man was pinned under his animal and struggling to pull his leg free.

Fury flooded through Fargo. He wished now he had shot the damn bear the moment he saw it. There it was, in a wild melee of men and horses, tearing into the rest of the party like a wolverine gone berserk. He snapped the Henry's stock to his shoulder but a plunging horse filled his sights and he jerked the rifle down again.

A woman wailed in terror.

Angeline Havard was desperately trying to rein her mare out of the bear's path but the petrified mare was slow to respond and paid a fearful cost for its fright.

Roaring in bestial bloodlust, the black bear raked the mare from shoulder to belly, its claws shredding hide and flesh and ripping wide. The mare whinnied and frantically sought to escape.

In a bound the bear had its jaws clamped on the mare's neck.

Angeline screamed. She pushed against her saddle to throw herself clear but the mare stumbled and went down. Her yellow hair flying, Angeline pitched hard to the ground. But she was up on her hands and knees in a twinkling.

The black bear saw her. It let go of the mare's throat and started to clamber over the mare to get at Angeline.

Fargo flew past McKern. The old man hollered something about "blowing out that damn varmint's wick." Fargo didn't catch all of it. He raised the Henry and took aim as best he could with the Ovaro moving under him, fixing a bead on the back of the black bear's head. Not an ideal shot, given how thick bear skulls were, but he must divert its attention from Angeline.

The bear's maw gaped wide and it went to leap on the helpless girl.

Fargo fired, worked the lever, fired again.

With a roar of pain, the bear spun and hurtled toward him.

Fargo hauled on the reins and brought the stallion to a slewing stop. He fired a third and a fourth time.

The bear didn't slow.

Quickly, Fargo took better aim. He had a front-on shot. He might be able to hit a lung or the heart but the slug had to go through a lot of muscle and fat.

He fired at its eyes, instead.

The Henry held fifteen rounds. He had already squeezed off six; now he squeezed off two more.

The bear became an ursine blur of fangs, claws, and hair.

Fargo banged off another shot.

Slowing, the bear shook its head, as a man might at the stings of a bee. Suddenly it reared onto its hind legs, and kept coming.

Which suited Fargo just fine; he had the heart and lung shots he wanted.

He fired, fired, fired, the Henry kicking with every blast.

Behind him McKern's Sharps thundered.

The Ovaro, superbly trained, stayed perfectly still. Its eyes were wide and its nostrils were flaring but it didn't bolt.

Fargo had lost count of his shots but he knew he only had one or two left. Another moment, and the bear would be on him. Its eyes were dark pits of animal hate.

That was when Rohan ran up. Rohan, filthy as sin, filthy clothes and filthy skin, with his fancy English shotgun he told everyone he won in a poker game. Rohan, the man in charge of the packhorses. He pointed his shotgun at the black bear's head and blew the top of the bear's skull off.

For a few seconds the bear stayed erect. That was how long it took the body to react to the fact it no longer had a brain. Over it keeled, hitting the ground with a thud, gore oozing from the cavity in its cranium.

Rohan puffed on the wisps of smoke rising from the muzzle of his shotgun, and chortled. "Did you see that? This baby of mine would drop an elephant."

"Seen a lot of elephants, have you?" Fargo had seen one once, with a traveling circus. The thing nearly killed him.

"No. But I ain't ignorant. I know what elephants are."

Fargo had forgotten how prickly the man could be. "Don't get your dander up. You did just fine."

"I'd have been here sooner but some of the packhorses tried to run off, and I figured saving our food and our bullets was more important than saving any of you."

"Don't let the man who hired us hear you say that."

"Hear him say what?" Theodore Havard demanded, striding up with his spare frame rigid and his shoulders thrown back, as was his habit. He had the air of a man who owned the world. In reality, he owned most of San Francisco.

"We were talking about that," Fargo said with a nod at the dead black bear. "Where were you in all the commotion?"

"My horse threw me and ran off. It's fortunate I wasn't trampled or broke a bone."

"Two of the men were mauled."

"They were? I didn't notice."

The rest were gathering. There was Edith Havard, Theodore's shrewish wife. There was Allen, twenty-five and unmarried. Shapely Angeline, younger by four years, brushing grass from her dress.

As for the hirelings, besides Fargo and McKern and Rohan there were eight others. Or six, if the two prone figures and the spreading pools of blood under them were any indication.

McKern came up, reloading his Sharps. "I have half a mind to shoot this damn critter again. It killed my horse, and I had that animal going on six years now."

"That a shame," Rohan said. "A good horse is special. Hell, any horse is better than people."

"Better how?" McKern responded.

"I'd rather sleep with a horse than a person any day."

McKern took a step back. "Has anyone ever told you that you're a mite weird?"

Of all of them, Allen Havard was the least flustered. He sat his expensive saddle, immaculate in a riding outfit that cost more than most men earned in a year, and sniffed in distaste. "Are you two buffoons done?"

"Sorry, Mr. Havard," McKern said.

Allen smirked at his father. "I knew it would come to this. I just knew it. I told you, didn't I, before we ever left home?"

"Don't start, boy," Theodore said sternly.

"I'm a *man*, Father, and I'll thank you to treat me like one."

"Must we bicker like this in public?" Edith asked.

Rohan drew a hunting knife and hunkered next to the black bear. He pried its mouth open and began to dig at the gums.

"My word!" Edith exclaimed. "What in heaven's name do you think you're doing?"

"This critter doesn't need its teeth anymore. I aim to make them into a right smart necklace."

Allen Havard uttered a sharp bark that passed for a laugh. "You should have listened to me, Father. I just hope to God this isn't an omen. If it is, we're all doomed."

No other series packs this much heat!

THE TRAILSMAN

**Follow the trail of the gun-slinging heroes of
Penguin's Action Westerns at
penguin.com/actionwesterns**

"A writer in the tradition of Louis L'Amour
and Zane Grey!"
—*Huntsville Times*

National Bestselling Author
RALPH COMPTON

**Available wherever books are sold or at
penguin.com**